# FOLLOW THE BLOODY BRICK ROAD

# Follow the Bloody Brick Road

MARK TARRANT

4 Horsemen
Publications, Inc.

Published By: 4 Horsemen Publications, Inc.

4 Horsemen Publications, Inc.
PO Box 417
Sylva, NC 28779
4horsemenpublications.com
info@4horsemenpublications.com

Cover Illustration by Raymond Noviar Witanto
Typesetting by Autumn Skye
Edited by Kris Cotter



Library of Congress Control Number: 2025932341

Paperback ISBN-13: 979-8-8232-0828-4
Hardcover ISBN-13: 979-8-8232-0829-1
Audiobook ISBN-13: 979-8-8232-0831-4
Ebook ISBN-13: 979-8-8232-0830-7

# TABLE OF CONTENTS

# CHAPTER 1

## "RAIN OF THE FORGOTTEN SOULS"

The ominous gray clouds cast soft shadows across the battlefield below. Thunder lightly rolled and lightning danced, transforming the color of the dark to hues of purple and blue electric light. The battle below was much like the torrid skies above, strong but drawing to an end.

This was no battle on our world of earth, but a battle in a world that was worlds away.

It was a battle of hope, of freedom. But in the shadows of the great clouds and rain, hopes were being crushed one after another, as one soldier fell every few seconds as they were slaughtered across a wet forest thick with mud.

The humans were aided by the greatest ironworking dwarves in the land. They had constructed "him" to lead the army to victory over an ominous, tyrannical foe. The leader the dwarves had constructed from iron and steel was named Achilles Swift Axe, General of the Iron Soldiers. The technology of the greatest human and dwarven minds had built the army of Iron Soldiers using steam to power great hulking machines. They were powerful, quick, and ten times stronger than the strongest human their world had ever seen. This new technology scared many, and though many were fearful of the new ways of motorized and steam engines over horse and cart, the machines were slowly growing into their world helping humans and sending the past of magic, myth, and the old ways deeper into the past.

It was this past that seemed hell-bent on refusing to relinquish control.

The Witch of the North and her demonic trees wrought destruction across the land with the aid of dark magic. She swore magic and the ancient ways were only for the good of the land, and thus war had ravaged the world.

There was one man who swore otherwise.

Only General Achilles and his mercenary mechanical army could stand up against the dark witch and her evil hordes. He stood like a juggernaut, his iron body gleaming as the clouds shadowed the sun. Rain pelted his hulking form as steam gears turned and creaked like a steam locomotive churning at full speed on a flat, open track. In his hand, he wielded his weapon, the great axe Sun Seeker.

"Fight on, Iron Soldiers! Do not let the trees take you!" his metallic voice cried out over the din of destruction.

The trees were an evil, dominating force the witch used to run off humans and dwarves alike. Their great, thick wooden bodies and flaying branchlike arms were swift in battle. They ripped down anything in the path, dragging their roots across the blood- and mud-soaked land. The witch had a plan to take the Diamond City and enslave humans and the dwarves as well. She had taken the Ruby City, ruled the Emerald City, and forced the dwarves of the last generation back into the Mountains of Mayhem, near the Iron Mountain.

The Diamond City was the remaining free city, the last stronghold against the witch. If the Diamond City fell, the world would be enslaved, and the age of man, machine, and technology would be gone forever. The world of magic, myth, and ancient gods would endure under the witch's twisted rule.

It would be a world of naught but the witch's will. So, the battle lines were drawn as dwarf, human, and iron soldiers fought on a hilly, wet, sloppy field outside the forest of light.

One last stand against her power-hungry soul.

The enemies of humankind, the haunting trees, resurrected warriors, and flying demonic creatures began to fall back. Then came a loud clap of thunder that could not but inspire awe. And suddenly the heavens opened. It rained unlike any downpour before. It was a flooding rain.

An angry rain of dark magic.

The humans and their allies could no longer see as the rain poured so heavily. It was at that moment when the trees regrouped and attacked once more. Wave after wave of trees and rain followed as men and dwarves stumbled in the mayhem of the downpour. Men and dwarves gasped and faltered and drowned. The storm howled as the resurrected dead warriors of the witch pushed forward in a staggering assault past the field, cutting down the humans and dwarves, who remained as the monstrous trees hurled bodies in the storm's wake.

The leader of the trees was Black Root, a commander under the evil witch. Standing nearly twenty feet tall and thick as the mightiest oak, Black Root advanced, ripping the limbs off the Iron Soldiers and humans alike. The Iron Soldiers would advance, fall back, and regroup, trying their best to protect the humans and dwarves who brought them to life.

"Don't retreat, my brothers!" Achilles yelled as he slammed his axe into the trunk of a tree, who howled in pain. "Bring them down!"

The humans and dwarves fired flaming arrows, but the wind and rain sent them cold, wet, and useless into their enemies. Their torches all extinguished, causing even more darkness and mayhem.

Iron Soldiers fell to the side in the mud, oil, and blood-covered soil on the battlefield. Achilles raised his axe and beheld what he had feared most. He and his troops were rusting. He watched as his army dwindled. The downpour had finally overpowered them, as weapons of fire were useless against the trees. Flaming arrows sputtered out after being launched and catapults of coal and fire proved of little worth on impact of soil or enemy.

The witch held the upper hand after seven days of rain. Her enemy forces were finally breaking. Achilles, however, ran into the heat of the battle with a vitriolic war cry. The ground shook with his thunderous charge beneath his thick iron legs. He swung his axe over and over, splitting trees in the body and face, sap spraying from each deep blow. He would take as many with him as he could, even if it meant the power cell in his forged chest burned out forever.

On a hill above the muddy battlefield, the evil witch smiled as she watched the battle from her campsite. Nearly three centuries old, the Witch of the North had watched the world change from a land of magic to a land of machines where humans, dwarves, and other creatures no longer needed magic—they were slowly gaining freedom from the old ways. A renaissance of science and free thinking had taken hold and was destroying the way their world had been for eons. The witch's power, and the power of all those reliant on magic, was now threatened.

The Witch of the North was as cunning as she was beautiful, and some say it was both that led to the death of the other witches and the remaining guardians of magic to disappear. As she took more power, men began to look toward new ways and no longer depend on the ways of old. In all truthfulness, it was her quest for power that made this war inevitable, but even with magic and great power, some refuse to acknowledge their folly. She had killed all her enemies quietly and swiftly. No band of humans, dwarves, others of magic, and their new machines would stop her last hold to rule the land and make it hers forever. Her dark purple eyes squinted, watching the fray in the rain and wind.

"You see how they grow weary?" she said calmly.

Standing to her left was a tall, thin creature wearing a black pointed cap and a brown cloth sack over his head. His eyes were deep blue through the eyeholes, and a slit in the sack revealed his teeth were gritted and grim. Straw jutted from underneath his sacklike mask. He was holding back fear and anger as one hand twitched.

"I told you we will win this war and take the Diamond City from the humans once and for all!" she boasted.

"You have deceived me," the brown cloth sack-draped figure replied. "I want no part of this butchery. You said only the Iron Soldiers would be destroyed and we would work with the humans and dwarves."

"Oh, you are so soft-hearted scareman," the witch laughed. "You know this is what we both desired. We would keep the last of magic for us alone. You did not seem to feel this was so dark and deceptive in my bed-chamber these last few months... Now enjoy the battle, for tomorrow we take the Diamond City. If you continue to question me, however, I may not use the magic of your book to return you once more to a human body. You may be made of straw forever!" she threatened.

The witch turned and grabbed the scareman by the mask with her pale fingers. "If we were not so close, and I didn't find you so deeply amusing, you might find yourself waking to find a lit torch in your bed of straw." She then pushed him back and returned to view the battle.

The scareman looked down at his hands. He wore black gloves, and straw poked from his wrists. He clenched his right hand in anger but then released. He lifted his head and watched in horror as humans and dwarves continued to be slaughtered in the storm of the rain.

"Wizard," she said to the scareman. "Do not take my threats lightly. I enjoyed our time together, but now is not the time to test my loyalty. Do not lose your mettle on me when we are so close to what we both desire."

The scareman watched on as he realized he had been a fool, a great fool indeed.

Down on the battlefield, the humans scattered, the dwarves fought on, and only five Iron Soldiers remained. The five Iron Soldiers formed a circle, back-to-back holding axes, iron staffs, and swords as the trees continued their advance. Rust had formed on all as they fought a hopeless battle. Their joints creaked and whined as their iron bodies continued to fight on, as bravery was one of their mightiest attributes.

"Achilles!" one shouted. "We must fall back! We can retreat to the city walls and return once more to fight in the sun! It cannot rain forever!"

"No! Brave Hammer, we must fight on! This is the witch's rain! The sun is gone! So, fight to see it once more!" Achilles ordered.

"We need more troops, the rust is taking over, we can barely move, we are..." Brave Hammer began as a branchlike arm grabbed him by the neck, ripping his forged head loose and tossing his mechanical body to fall on the muddy ground.

"No!" Achilles yelled as he leaped into the air, steam shooting from his rusting joints, and sent Sun Seeker into the oak monster, splitting him in half.

"I was not created to die in a losing battle!" Achilles screamed. "I was created to lead to victory!"

An older Dwarf leaped through the air and sank his axe into a nearby resurrected warrior, separating its head from its body.

"Achilles, we have to fall back!" he shouted. "The lions will surely come to our aid!"

"No! The Isle of the Lions damned us since they betrayed their treaty with you! They left us to die here this day!"

The dwarf swore under his breath and ran back into the fight, swinging his axe.

The trees surrounded the four remaining Iron Soldiers as the clouds darkened, thunder boomed, and rain poured ever more heavily on the remaining Iron Soldiers.

"I refuse to fall to you demons!" Achilles cried, swinging his axe in a furor.

The rain continued, as did the onslaught of men and dwarves.

The witch looked at the scareman. His eyes still glistened as the slaughter continued. He swallowed hard.

It would be the end of machines, and magic would no longer be used for good.

It was his fault, and the fault of that damned book. His obsession with power had taken his face and skin, burned him so badly he was forced to hide under masks and gloves. His gain of magic and power had made him a slave to hiding himself and an outcast amongst men.

Now she had the book, and he was just a pawn as he realized his fate was that of those on the battlefield.

"Do you see the one called Achilles?" the witch asked. "The last machine fighting... a great machine built to save their world. They say he is different from the others... almost as if magic fueled him. It is rumored his powers are forged from magic below the fires of the Black Mountain. No matter... He fights well in the fray, but it is too late. He has accepted his fate. I told Dark Root to take him alive... I wish to make an example out of him. Now come," the witch snarled, "let us finish this mockery of a rebellion."

The witch, the scareman, and her resurrected warrior bodyguards trudged slowly down the muddy hillside to the bloodied field below as the fighting slowed. Men and dwarves cried out but were quickly silenced as blows fell and fell upon them, and the rain continued to fall.

## "HOLD THE ONIONS"

Our Universe: Earth, Kansas—10 years later

Down a small stretch of lonesome highway in a dusty dirt parking lot, a quaint little diner sat on the edge of town—Happy Burger Cafe. A large billboard with its name and a woman in a tight pink dress holding a plate with a hamburger and French fries had faded over time at the edge of the property. The diner had been there since the end of World War II, the billboard since 1975. By now it felt as if it had always been there for anyone turning off the slow interstate road needing a meal, pie for a church picnic, or fried chicken dinner for friends who were coming over and you had nothing to feed them.

It was a staple in a time of years past, but seventy-plus years later, time can pass such things by. Nevertheless, this little diner in a time of cell phones and video games still clung to life near one of the closest small farming towns in Kansas. It sat quietly as cars and trucks pulled into its dirt parking lot. The diner was chrome, with white and black checkered trim and a screen door to greet you, the smell of its home cooking drifting toward eager diners. A police car barreled down the road and quickly turned into the dirt parking lot. The officer got out and walked into the diner with his hat under his arm. The screen door made a creek as it closed behind him.

"Well, if it isn't Officer Rollins," a woman's voice noted. "Is it Thursday already, Officer?"

Officer Rollins, a young officer with short black hair and a chiseled jaw, smiled at the older woman with gray and brown hair wrapped tight in a bun behind the counter.

"Yes, Mrs. Mable, it is. Can I have the usual?"

"Anything you want. You want extra fries with the steak? I tried something new…"

"Oh, that would be more than fine," Officer Rollins replied.

"Better watch out for her new ideas, Henry." A tall lanky man spoke as he stood up from the counter and put out his hand.

"How ya been? Haven't seen ya around lately."

Officer Rollins shook his strong hand. Bill's left arm was missing from the elbow down, and his flannel shirt was pinned right below where his arm should be.

"Good, Bill, and you? How is the farming coming along? I mean, is it farming or cultivating? I never can remember."

"I've been losing a lot of business. Folks are movin' out. They don't wanna deal with the weather every few years. This dry spell has been hard on everybody. Kansas can be a very unforgiving state some years. Drought, tornadoes, it ain't an easy place to try to squeak out a living. Thank God I became a pot farmer."

"Just think, four years ago, I may have arrested you. Now I can just sit back and let you work your magic."

"Times change, and life is funny sometimes... not that you could arrest me. I got a good lawyer."

"I never doubted it," the officer said and smiled. "Anyway, I think it's gonna pass—all the odd weather. It has to change. Maybe it's all that global warming those city folks always yammer on about. We have a bet down at the station on it. A whole pool based on when it's going to rain again."

"I hope it's soon, and you win big," Bill stated. He sat back and looked at his plate. "Hey, Mable, are these onion rings or what? Well, what are they? Damn woman tryin' new things to keep up with city folks!" He took his fork and flipped something away from his French fries. Henry smiled as he found a booth and sat down.

Just then, a young woman wearing a pair of tight blue jeans and a white t-shirt with a flannel wrapped around her waist bolted through the screen door. Her long auburn hair hung over her green eyes, made unmanageable by the heat. She walked quickly by the counter.

"Sorry I'm late, Auntie. My car broke down, and I was late for my classes," she hurriedly explained as she grabbed an apron and ran into the kitchen. Seconds later, she emerged with a baseball cap on, keeping her hair in control, and tried to adjust her apron.

"I had to borrow Bob's truck. It's been crazy, but I'm here."

"That's fine, dear," Mable said. "It's slow today, so no bother."

The young woman walked over to Henry's table and poured him a glass of water.

"Morning, Dorothy." Henry smiled. "How are things?"

"Good, I guess. Just working and taking some classes at the community college."

"Hey, I heard Bob Taylor and you got engaged? I never thought he would settle down. I remember him always makin' trouble, even before I left for the academy." He laughed.

"No, he works hard. He has a small construction business. It's been kinda slow recently, though. He had a big job today, but one of his buddies was gonna pick him up."

"Well, I'm glad for you," Henry said and took a long drink of iced water. The glass was ice cold and had sweat sliding down its sides.

The sound of the screen door opened, and a man with his sleeves rolled up, wearing a green and black flannel shirt, walked in with a strut. He had short, blond, spiked hair and a pair of hard-worn jeans. He looked around and gave a quick nod to Bill at the counter.

Dorothy didn't acknowledge him much and leaned down and looked at Henry.

"Look, it's the town hero, Allen Abrams, all-star linebacker. Gonna put the town on the map everyone said... Then he blew out his knee just before the NFL draft," Dorothy said shrewdly. "That guy thought he was gonna be something. Now he's cuttin' wood for a living for his old man at their sawmill."

"Ah, come on, Dorothy. I went to school with him. He wasn't such a jerk, just an egomaniac. He's been through a lot. I heard he was having some new surgery to try for a comeback."

"Oh, please! Give me a break," Dorothy whispered.

Allen walked over and looked at Henry.

"Hey, Henry. How's it goin'? You still playing Dirty Harry?"

"Sure am. People love to make my day... How about you?"

"Good, training and workin'. How's your job? Hey, did you hear Missy Glenn moved outta town?"

"Yeah, she was so pretty. I remember the prom when Travis and I got so hammered one night, and..."

"Well, boys," Dorothy interrupted, "I'll let you relive your glory days. Some of us have work to do..." Dorothy smirked and walked away.

"Man, she can be rude!" Allen said

"Naw, she's a nice girl, not like the ones we used to park with," Henry said, smiling. "Besides, she has a lot going on. Her dad passed away last winter, and her aunt, who owns this place, is getting heat from the bank. The lack of rain the last couple years just about broke the whole damn town."

"Yeah, I know. My dad said it was the worst he's seen in twenty years. The lumber business is taking a real beating with the fires, too." Allen paused. "Can I join ya for a quick bite?"

"Sure," Henry said.

Allen joined Henry at the red vinyl booth. It was a bit uncomfortable, but after a couple adjustments, Allen found a spot that didn't hurt his back or sink under his large frame. The diner had seen better days, that was for sure. They soon got their meals as they laughed and reminisced about their "Glory Days." Dorothy brought them their checks and walked back to the register. She gazed out the big open bay window past the red etched lettering and looked out to the dirt roads, highway, and dying cornfields. The sun had pushed its light hard on this small community the last few months.

Her mind thought of the last time it had rained, and to her despair, she found could not recall it. As she was looking, a black BMW pulled into the dirt parking lot, braking hard and spilling clouds of dust into the dry summer air.

"Oh man," Dorothy mumbled. "Aunt Mable, we've got trouble. It's Miss Harris from the bank again."

Mable emerged from the kitchen and walked out front. She adjusted her apron, more because of nerves than anything else.

"Oh, Lord. This is not what I need," she said.

A tall, thin woman in a black business suit strolled in with a stride more affectation than anything else—replete with a briefcase in her hand. She had dark eyes and thin lips. Her hair was black and hung just below her ears. The screen door creaked closed, almost as if the creak were an announcement or warning.

"Well, Mable, we have been fair, but three months is it. The Westbrook Bridge Bank simply cannot hold out on your loans."

The woman then set her briefcase on the counter and popped it open.

"Listen, you need to sell or claim bankruptcy. I hear Burger Town might be interested in this location," the woman said with a smirk.

"I told you last month I'm not selling! We've had this place for nearly gosh-darn fifty years! Give me an extension. One more month, please. I can try to give you the three months back payments then, I swear..." Mable pleaded.

"Sorry, my hands are tied. It's not my fault you had to take out a loan to save it ten years ago. You have two weeks; then we auction. Here are all the papers if you have any questions." The woman set them on the counter and looked at Mable. "You're lucky to get that. I could still sue you for that chicken I ate a few months ago on my last visit. I was sick for two days." She looked into the kitchen. "I bet I could close you down with health violations alone..."

Dorothy felt heat creep up her neck and into her face, and finally she could hold back no more. "That chicken was fine. Maybe you just have real bad PMS."

Allen and Henry both laughed, and Bill from his booth grinned as he sipped his lukewarm coffee.

"Listen, child, go in the back, do your dishes, and come see me in five years when you have any kind of an education. Something more than a GED," Miss Harris said with a smirk.

"I graduated three years ago, thank you. I am taking law at Greenfield Community College," Dorothy replied.

The banker stood up and looked down at Dorothy. Her lips curled. "Good for you for applying yourself, not that it'll matter in this town. But right now, remember... you're just a girl working at a run-down diner."

Dorothy's heart sank, and she adjusted her apron.

Miss Harris fixed her hair with a shrewd smile and looked down at Bill, who sipped his coffee.

"William," she said with a short smile through thin lips.

"Good afternoon, Clair," he said almost friendly.

"Saw you the other day in town ... by the bank."

"Yeah, picking up some supplies... No need to go to the bank. I ain't behind on anything since I sold off a lot of the farm, just me now and a few acres. Gotta good crop of Mary Jane coming in now though. No more corn and beans for this one-armed fella. All my plants are in greenhouses, so Mother Nature can't touch me, unlike my neighbors. Got all my papers and plenty of buyers up in Kansas City."

She was about to speak, but then came a small pause as she realized she was not needed. He was done with her, and she felt useless, but managed to feign confidence.

"Well, if you ever want to come in and talk about restructuring or need a car loan or anything... just pop in and ask."

"I will. Truck is fine, land is holding out." He looked up, smiled at her and sipped his coffee again. She looked around the empty diner. The air was still. She had lost her air of authority, so she returned to the attack.

"Well, it's no wonder you can't make your payments, Mable, one cop from town, a run-down football star, an old pot grower, and such bad pie... it's no wonder you can't keep this diner in the black." She then giggled lightly.

No one said a word.

"Well, I know when I've worn out my welcome. Ta ta, all." The woman turned and opened the screen door just as a black dog shot in. He shook as he entered, sending dirt and sand on the unwelcome guest.

"Damn it! I may just call the Board of Health! There's a dog in the restaurant? Oh, yeah... I'll be back." She stormed out.

Dorothy kneeled and began to pet the dog, a muscular Rottweiler. His brown eyes were sad.

"Sorry, Conan," she said. "I know it's hot out there. I'll get ya some water."

"What a witch that woman is." Allen sighed.

"No kidding! She gets a little power and money and turns into a leech. She knows how hard things are. She grew up in this town. She just wants more. How much they spend on the new bank?"

"Hey, Bill, how long did you date her?" Henry said with a smirk.

Bill's face fell flat. "It was years ago, and I was coming off being a widow, and we both had a fondness for whiskey. We all make mistakes... In my defense, she looked pretty darn good wearing only my work boots, a cowboy hat, and a flannel shirt! Anyway, like I said, that was years ago... she fooled me good. I was foolish enough to think she was different than most folks claimed. I was a fool."

Dorothy looked at her aunt. "What are we going to do about the bank?"

"I don't know, honey. I can't see a way of saving this place."

"Wait! I have an idea. I'll go see Bob. He was left some money when his uncle passed. We were setting some apart for the wedding and honeymoon... Maybe I can convince Bob that we can afford to lend it to you! Hell," she said as she took off her apron, "we're engaged, we're family, and family looks after its own."

"No, Dorothy! I can't borrow anymore... Not that it's not a kind offer, sweetheart," Her aunt stated.

"No, don't worry. I'll get it," Dorothy said as she bolted from the door.

"Come on, boy, let's go." The dog joined his master and jumped into the old green pickup, and the two sped off the lot, sending dust and dirt into the dry air.

"Damn girl! She won't listen. She's just like her father, stubborn as a mule," Mable said. Bill looked over at Mable.

"Well, a little fire is good in a woman. She sure is tough. Suppose she needed to be growin' up with no mom and two brothers... She's a tomboy, that's for sure."

"Just drink your coffee," Mable said and walked back into the kitchen, rubbing her temples. "What a day!"

Henry got up, and Allen followed him to the register. "I wish there was a way to keep that horrible woman from taking over this town," Henry said as he pulled bills out of his wallet. "I figure I'll buy a few pieces of pie for the guys back at the station. Ya know, maybe that's an idea— have a pie fundraiser. Like a bake sale. Everyone loves her pie. She's won the last four years at the county fair."

Allen looked around but could not see Mable any-where. "Where did she go?"

The two young men waited by the register, but no one came. They looked around the doorway into the kitchen and saw Mable at a desk, her head down.

She was sobbing.

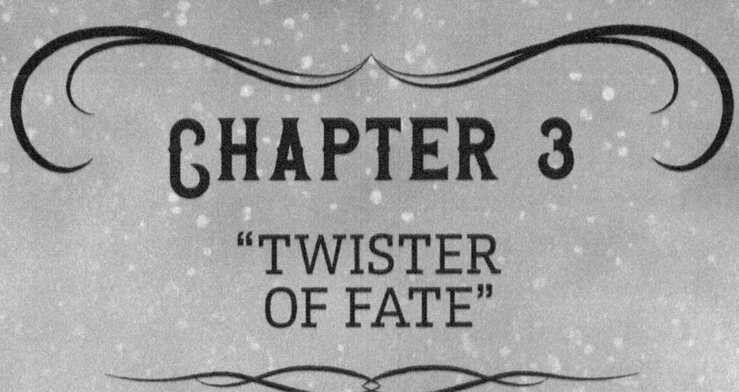

# CHAPTER 3

## "TWISTER OF FATE"

The winds blew wildly as the green truck raced down the county road. Dorothy watched ahead as tumbleweeds and shrubs blew by the windshield. She turned on the radio as "All My Exs Live in Texas" came on. She looked over to Conan. "Rough weather, aye, boy?"

The dog licked his lips as he also stared out the window. Dorothy picked up her cell phone, hit a button, and listened. No answer. Suddenly the phone vibrated as the screen brightened. She glanced at it, hoping it was Bob, but it wasn't. An ad popped on the screen.

"Kill the witch and save the world!" it read. Beneath the text, a castle stood silent, and there was a pile of coins near the front gate.

"Stupid game. You download it, play it a few times, and they hit you up for more money to keep playing." She then slid the phone into her front pocket, trying to concentrate on the road.

"Hell, I'll just run over to Bob's place. See if he's there," she said and turned up the radio.

Several minutes later, she turned off the main road and slowly turned into a gravel driveway that led to a large white trailer house with dark green shutters. As she approached, she noticed a red late-model Mustang. "I didn't think any of Bob's buddies had a sports car," she murmured to herself.

She quickly dismissed her curiosity and parked the truck. She ran to the door and tried to open it. It was locked. She knocked loudly and waited. The wind was picking up as leaves and dust blew past the porch. Conan just looked out the truck window. The door opened, and she squeezed inside quickly.

"My God, Bob! What took so long?" Dorothy asked. "It's getting nasty out there."

"Oh, I'm sorry," Bob replied, looking a little red in the face as he looked around nervously.

Dorothy walked over to the couch, plopped down, and let out a sigh. "Wow! It's really coming down," she said.

"Um... yeah," he answered.

"Hey, I thought you had some big job today?" Dorothy said as she looked out at the red Mustang.

"Oh, we decided to wait until tomorrow. This weather just caught us by surprise—things are supposed to clear up tomorrow, though."

"Whose car is that out there?"

"Oh, that? I'm borrowing it from Dale..."

"Dale?"

"Yeah, he gets me tools at a discount. Haven't I mentioned him to you?" As he finished his statement, a woman with long, wet blonde hair in a dark green towel walked from the hallway.

"Hey, lover, do have any—" She looked at Dorothy, "Ooh... Sorry, didn't know you had company."

Dorothy looked at the woman in shock and then looked at Bob.

"Oh my God! I mean... I have to go..." Dorothy jumped up and ran from the living room.

"Dorothy, wait!" Bob called out, but Dorothy was already outside as Bob ran after her. She flung open the door to the truck and jumped in. Bob stood on the small wooden porch, calling after her. Dorothy quickly rolled down the truck window.

"How could you? You bastard!" she yelled. She ripped the engagement ring from her finger and threw it at Bob. "Give it to your little shower buddy, you son of a bitch!"

She started the truck, threw it into reverse, and floored the gas pedal. The truck fishtailed as it left the dirt and gravel driveway, spinning and sending rock, dust, and dirt everywhere. Dorothy slammed the truck into drive and put the pedal almost through the floor, disappearing down County Road 105.

The woman in the towel came to the door.

"I thought she was gonna be at work," she asked.

"Well, you were in the shower. I had no way of stopping her from coming in, not in this storm."

"Well, that's fine... It's over! Now we can be together!"

Bob's face turned white. "She has my truck and all my tools!"

"Sweetie, it's okay; it's just us now."

Bob walked off the porch and looked down the highway.

"My truck... my truck," he stuttered.

"That son of a bitch!" Dorothy screamed as tears streaked her face. "Two years! I gave him two years..." She wiped the tears from her eyes as Conan tried to lick her face to comfort her.

"No, down, boy! Damn it!"

She slammed her fist on the steering wheel and turned up the radio as she looked at the rainy road ahead. The song on the radio cut short as an emergency warning blared. *"Severe high winds are building; this is a tornado warning... People are advised to stay home!"*

"Yeah, whatever." Rage had slowed her thoughts to a trickle.

"Ya know what, Conan... I should total his truck! Wait a second... I could sell all the tools and stuff to a pawnshop. Ha! I like that idea! That's how we save the diner; we pawn all the tools and then sell his truck!" She laughed as she drove. The winds seemed to blow harder, and she slowed down.

"I gotta get off the road and get home quick smart. After the weather gets better, we can drive out to Lincoln City, pawn all the tools we can, and bring Mable the money. That's the plan... that son of a bitch!" she yelled once more.

"You know what they say, there's no place like home... Well, if you have a good one, that is." She turned off the station on the radio and concentrated on the road ahead.

Conan barked.

"What is it, boy? I know it's bad, just sit tight. We'll get home. I swear."

Dust, weeds, and rocks were now blowing once again across the windshield, giving her a limited view. Then, to her horror, she saw it... a twister, a dark swirling mass just a mile ahead.

"Oh my God!" she said as she slowly put on the brakes. The truck slowed and finally stopped with a small screech. She turned the truck around and pushed the pedal to the floor.

"Hold on, Conan!"

She looked in the rearview mirror as the tornado grew ever closer.

"Not today... not today of all days. No, no..." Dorothy yelled and kept the pedal to the floor.

The wild mass of winds and dirt gained, however, and the truck began to shake.

"I know I can outrun this thing," Dorothy said to comfort herself.

Then there was a loud pop. The truck fell to one side as the front tire blew out, spinning the truck out of control. Dorothy screamed as the truck slid wildly. She tried slamming on the brakes, but the truck still slid off the road and into a small gully.

The impact slammed her head into the driver's side door. Dorothy gripped the wheel tightly, looking around in a panic. She was fine, for now, it seemed. The truck was still and quiet.

And then, "Oh my God!" she shouted.

Conan whimpered on the floorboard. Dorothy put her head on the wheel and tried to regain her composure. Thunder echoed behind her. She glanced up and saw the twister sweeping toward her in the rearview mirror.

She looked out the window in time to see it approach like a dark phantom. She tried to start the truck, but it just sputtered and whined.

The truck began to shake.

Dorothy looked up one last time.

"Oh, dear God!" she screamed as the truck lifted from the ground. She felt like she was floating and screamed once more. The truck began to spin as it lifted off the road higher and higher into the massive twister.

Dorothy screamed one final time as her body was tossed and shaken. Her head slammed into the steering wheel. She went limp, and the truck flew out of control, caught up in the mighty twister.

# CHAPTER 4

## "DEFINITELY NOT IN KANSAS"

Dorothy felt a wet, slick object smear across her cheek. She mumbled as Conan licked her wildly. She was numb all over and tried to move her toes and then tried opening her eyes. At first, everything was blurry, especially as Conan was licking every inch of her face.

"No, Conan, down, boy," she mumbled. She tried focusing on the steering wheel. This took close to a minute, but she finally could see her surroundings. She heard a ringing in her ears, and her head pounded like the world's worst hangover. She sat up and looked into the back of the cab at the collection of tools. She looked into the rearview mirror and saw a cut above her left eye. The gun rack still held a shotgun.

"Damn, we're lucky to still be alive, boy," she said to Conan, who lay close as if protecting his master.

"Okay, okay... I'm okay," she repeated to herself. She then groaned as she pushed the door open and nearly fell from the truck. Her body ached all over. Dorothy grabbed the door as she gained her composure and looked around. There were fields... several dead trees and mountains for miles.

"Mountains?" she whispered as she looked around at the landscape. It was very dark and gray. No rain at all, but the clouds seemed frozen in the sky. Conan bounded from the truck cab and sniffed around.

"Where the hell are we?" she murmured. She looked at the sky once more. "Where is the sun?"

Conan began to bark and leap around. "What is it, boy?" Dorothy asked as she walked to the rear of the truck. Conan stood barking wildly as Dorothy saw what appeared to be a body underneath the rear right tire.

"Oh my God!" She ran over and kneeled down. It was then that she noticed the arm covered in fur and the hand with claws. "What the hell!" She stumbled back. The body wore a green robe with a black piece of cloth wrapped around the waist.

Dorothy couldn't see the head, as it was farther under the truck. She quickly went back into the cab, opened the glove box, and pulled out a small pistol. She made her way back to the corpse. As Conan sniffed the body, Dorothy kneeled to get a better view.

"We may have killed Big Foot, Conan. All those YouTube people will be thrilled. We have to call someone…"

She pulled her cell phone from her pocket and began to dial 911.

"No service," she said angrily. She walked a few steps waving her phone around, but no bars appeared. She let out a sigh and slid her phone back into her pocket.

"Seventy bucks a month for nothing!" she mumbled.

She cautiously peered under the truck and saw the monster's face. It resembled an ape, but with a larger jaw and rows of teeth. Its eyes were open, and its tongue lay out of its mouth.

"Damn," Dorothy said. "That is ugly. Why would Big Foot feel the need to wear clothes?"

She got back up and walked over to the cab of the truck. She looked at the front of the truck and the flat tire.

"Plan is the same, Conan, go and sell everything and save the diner, right, boy? Now let's see if Bob wasted all his money on guns or was smart enough to have a spare." She leaned inside and started to grab the keys in the ignition.

"A spare what?" asked a gruff voice. Dorothy spun around with the pistol pointed. She looked down. A short man dressed in rags looked up at her. He had a long scar down the left side of his face and a full gray beard and mustache.

"Oh my God! Sorry, you scared me," Dorothy stated as she pointed the weapon down toward the short man.

"I'm sorry, young lady. I meant no harm; I just wanted the keys." The intruder held up his hands. They were chained together.

"Keys?" Dorothy asked. "You break out of prison? Nearest prison is Clark County, forty miles away. Did that twister throw us forty miles? That's not possible," she said and looked at Conan, who sat wagging his nub of a tail.

"Some guard dog," she muttered, "letting this man creep up on us... and a wanted man at that."

"Yes, yes," the man said as he walked over to the corpse under the truck. "This big ape has the keys to our bonds. We can't escape without them." He felt around the corpse's robe and pulled out a ring of several silver keys. "See." The man smiled. "Now we can finally be free."

Dorothy looked around.

"Why do you keep saying we?" she asked, still pointing the gun at the intruder.

"Oh, yes... there are several of us," he said in a deep voice. "We were all in captivity under the witch, but you have given us our sweet, sweet freedom!"

Dorothy looked around as a couple dozen more little people came out of hiding. They all wore different colored rags, and all were indeed chained. Some of them were even chained to another. Dorothy aimed the gun at them, unsure what to do as they approached.

"We will not hurt you. We are in your debt," the man said. "I am Brawner Wild Hammer, chief of the Tribe of Dirkwood. We have been enslaved for nearly four years. You saved us!"

The small man held out his hand in a gesture to shake Dorothy's. She slowly reached out with one hand, still pointing the gun at the small crowd who had encircled her.

"Um, I'm Dorothy, from Cottonwood, Kansas... I think I'm lost," she stammered.

"Cottonwood, Kansas, eh? Some human town I'm sure," the man said. He walked over to another dwarf and handed him the keys. "Free our people! We will go back to the mountains and rejoin our dwarven kin after all these years!"

Dorothy looked around. Conan walked over and leaned against her, his butt still wiggling.

"Some guard dog," she repeated.

Brawner walked back over to Dorothy.

"My people will do all we can to help you return home, ma'am, but I have to admit I've never heard of this town—Cottonwood, Kansas... What is that machine behind you? How did it fall from the sky and kill our guard?"

Dorothy looked at the dwarves and then thought about home, Bob, and the tornado.

"Oh my God," she mumbled. "Oh, hell no..."

"What is it, child?"

"Okay," Dorothy began muttering to herself. "I'm Dorothy. I'm from Kansas. There was a tornado, and now I'm surrounded by little people whom I just accidentally freed after accidentally killing someone." Dorothy raised her gun, "Okay, you lil' bastards, I don't know what freaking game this is, or sick joke, but I want to see some cameras now! Is this some shit reality show? Did Bob put you up to this... or is this some stupid YouTube prank?"

The dwarves just stared blankly at her. Her hands shook as she held the gun. "Oh, man! This is not happening! No way!" She began to panic. "Okay, get a grip, Dorothy! Stay cool, just change the damn tire and drive outta here for good."

"Is something wrong?" Brawner asked.

"Nothing a spare tire and a few beers can't fix," she replied as she walked back to the truck. She opened the cab and pulled out a tire, a jack, and a wrench. She tried to carry them all and still point the pistol at the dwarves, but she dropped the wrench. Brawner politely picked it up and handed it back to her.

"Thanks," she said. "Um, I'm just going to fix my machine and get out of your hair..."

"Oh, okay. It's an awfully beautiful machine. They have outlawed all machines, so I've heard."

The dwarf turned to the others. "She's fine. Let's all go home. She doesn't seem to need our assistance."

"Wait! I didn't say that! I need to get home! I mean, where the hell am I?"

"You are in the land of the witch. At least now that's what our land is called," Brawner replied.

"This day has become stranger and stranger," Dorothy muttered as she threw the tire down.

"Oh, so you have heard of it?"

"No, I just know about it. It's a child's story... It's fiction! Trust me, I'm from Kansas. My name is Dorothy, blah, blah, blah. I get teased a lot, as you can guess... and I just need to get home," Dorothy said as she sighed, and her eyes began to moisten.

"I don't know if we can help you," Brawner said sadly.

"Oh wait! That's okay! I just have to find some wizard, get some red shoes, and click my heels. That is unless I wake up from this dream, right?" Dorothy said deliriously. "So, the story goes anyway... I'm probably not even here. Maybe I'm just dreaming." She felt the cut on her head as she said this, and it certainly hurt a lot.

"Dreams should not hurt, though. Something is not right," she whispered.

"Um," Brawner interrupted. "Wizard? There is no wizard. Well, not anymore, that is. He was slain after the battle in the Forest of the Damned... that was the rumor. Horrible man, he gave the witch our world."

"Okay," Dorothy paused in contemplation. "What about ruby slippers?"

"Why would anyone wear shoes made of rubies?"

Dorothy looked puzzled. "Oh no, this is not good, not at all. I'm having a nightmare. Yeah, I'm unconscious! This is a dream... That twister knocked me out... and now this." She looked around at the dead trees and the dwarves. It was very clear now that she was on her own. Fortunately, she had learned to adapt at a young age, be self-reliant, keep moving, always keep moving. She realized that she had better just stay cool before the panic resurfaced.

"Or," she continued, "I'm dead, and this is my own sick twisted hell." She quickly ran back to the cab of the truck and put the keys in the ignition. She turned on the radio, and static played out of the speakers. She moved the dial, searching for a voice, any voice, but none was found. She walked over, sat down next to the spare tire, put her head down, and started to cry.

"Now, come on, girl. Don't be sad. We will help you; we'll get your machine working and send you on your way," Brawner said, trying to comfort her. "We have to be quick, though. If the witch finds we have escaped, we'll all be killed."

Dorothy wiped the tears from her eyes and stood.

"Sure... witch, giant Big Foots in robes, bad dream... coma... hell... Whatever, let's get this done." *Always keep moving,* she thought. "I'll figure this out. Not sure how... but I will."

# CHAPTER 5

## "A DIM LIGHT IN A SEA OF DARKNESS"

The dwarves were very eager to help Dorothy and were in awe of her machine. Several ran and hid behind rocks as she started the engine. Dorothy looked through the cracked windshield and saw the dead world she was now in. Gray clouds stretched for miles. The air was cold and then warm when the breeze blew. You could smell the rain but could not see any. There was no sign of the sun whatsoever.

"I'm glad all I lost was the tire," she whispered to herself, "or I would be so damn screwed." She looked at the gas gauge; it was at a half tank. "Well, I might get somewhere, maybe."

Suddenly a dwarf ran from a nearby hill.

"The witch is coming! Hide, hide!" the little warrior yelled. Several of the dwarves fled, quickly scattering everywhere.

"Great," Dorothy said. A group of dwarves dove into the cab and fell into the back seat, shoving Dorothy over.

"Hey, what's the big idea?" she yelled.

Brawner looked at her. "If this machine can move, make it move now! And fast!"

"Okay," Dorothy said as she slammed down on the gas pedal. The truck flew from the small ditch onto a dirt road. Dorothy laughed in relief as the dwarves screamed. She looked up into her rearview mirror and saw what appeared to be a band of dark horses and armored guards cresting over a hillside. They slowly disappeared from sight as she pushed harder on the pedal.

"I hope the others got away," she said to Brawner.

"Me too, me too," the dwarf leader replied sadly.

The witch looked around and saw her monster guard sprawled out in the dirt. She looked over at a hulking, hairy beast with a slanted jaw and beady eyes. "Butcher..." the witch said evilly. "Whatever or whoever killed this guard left tracks. I want you to follow them. Take the flying creatures if you must, but I want whoever killed my guard and freed those puny dwarves brought to me directly!"

"Yes, my Queen," the creature growled. One of the witch's guards strode down a small hill carrying a struggling dwarf. The dwarf fought hard as he was dragged to the witch.

"Good work," the witch praised. "Let's see if the little runt has any brains at all, shall we?" The guard tossed the dwarf to the ground, and he bounced right to his feet.

"I am not afraid of you," he said loudly and confidently.

The witch smiled down at the fight-filled little captive. "Oh? You will be soon enough unless you tell me what happened here."

"I saw nothing!" The dwarf then spat into the witch's face. The witch retaliated by raising her hand and flicking her fingers. The dwarf spun, knocking him to the dirt.

"I have lost my patience with you! I gave you a chance, and now you will suffer before you die!"

The dwarf jumped up and tried to run away, but several of the witch's resurrected warriors deftly blocked his retreat. The witch grabbed the dwarf by the neck and looked into his green, watering eyes.

"You *will* tell me what I need to know," she threatened as she took her finger and slowly drew blood from his neck with her nail. The dwarf squirmed, but the witch cut deeper. Blood flowed heavily as the dwarf struggled. "Now... tell me what happened... and I swear I will kill you quickly."

The prisoner looked at the witch as the strength drained from his body.

"I saw ... a machine... it fell from the sky... and I saw a girl climb from the machine..." The dwarf's eyes began to tear more and more in shame.

"More! Tell me more!" she screamed.

The dwarf let out a gurgling sigh as his last breath. The witch threw the stocky body down. She wiped the spit from her face, grimaced, and took a deep breath.

"Okay, enough. You may feed."

Several of the resurrected warriors dove onto the dwarf, licking the blood from his neck, while others bit down on his fleshy arms.

"Butcher! I want this girl alive. As for the dwarves, kill them! Now go... and do not fail me!" the witch concluded with a threat.

The creatures nodded and began to follow the tire marks in the mud and sand. A dozen armored resurrected warriors staggered behind the shaggy beasts.

Dorothy drove for nearly thirty minutes when the truck came to a fork in the dirt road. "What... where are we? Where do we go?" Dorothy asked.

"Go to the right. I don't want you to visit the Forest of the Damned. We must head west to my brothers. We are very close to a safe area. We have dwarven kin nearby in these parts. Many dwarves still hide in the mountains from the witch and her army," he noted.

Dorothy looked ahead and saw the main road branch off.

"Well, if you think it will help. I just wanna get my ass outta here." Without warning, a rock struck the driver's window.

"What the hell?" Dorothy yelled as she started to accelerate as fast as possible. Several more rocks and spears bombarded the truck.

"We're under attack!" she screamed. Recovering from her shock, she went to hit the gas again, but the dwarven leader shouted out.

"No wait! They're dwarves. Hold on… stop your machine." Brawner jumped out of the truck and ran out in front of the vehicle.

"My kin, please stop this attack!" he yelled.

The rocks slowly stopped. As one last rock hit the windshield, Dorothy saw several more dwarves appear from behind rocks and fallen trees. Their clothing was tattered and worn. Many held spears and bows. One husky dwarf ran out to meet Brawner. When they met, they shook hands excitedly.

"Brawner, thank the maker, you live!" the dwarf shouted.

"Yes, I am still alive, my friend. Tell me, Orff, how long has it been?"

"Close to five years, I would imagine. What is this machine… and how did you manage to free yourselves? We raided the caves so many times to save you, but were always forced to retreat."

"I know you did," Brawner said. "Don't worry. Someone is here with a new machine from a distant land, and maybe she can help us."

Dorothy watched as the other dwarves jumped from the truck and met with the visitors.

Dorothy climbed from the truck and walked up to the two dwarves, interrupting the happy reunion. "Um, excuse me, I still have to get home."

"Dorothy, this is Orff 'Wild Axe'. He is my brother-in-law. Well," he said angrily, "he was until the witch tossed my sister into the Pit. We will stay with him tonight and eat and rest. Tomorrow, we will travel to our home inside the Iron Mountain. We will be safe there, and then I promise we will do all we can to send you home."

Dorothy looked at all the dwarves as they yelled and laughed. She was disappointed, but it was obvious how much joy and happiness the new freedom had given the dwarves.

"I am truly sorry about your problems, but I need to find a way home."

"Home?" Orff asked. "I thought all humans lived near the remains of the Ruby, Emerald, and Diamond Cities?"

"No, she is ... lost," replied Brawner. "She is not from our lands. We are going to help her all we can. After all, she and this machine gave us our freedom. It is the least we can do."

Brawner put his arm around Orff and looked at the dwarves. "My brothers," he announced loudly. "We rest tonight, and tomorrow we return to Iron Mountain!"

The dwarves let out a cheer. Dorothy rubbed her temples as her headache grew more painful.

Orff smiled and looked at Brawner. "I have a surprise for you, my brother."

"Really?"

"This morning, some from our clan went scouting to secure our area, and guess what we caught..."

"What?"

"Bring out the prisoner!" Orff ordered.

Several dwarves dragged out a figure of a man. He was clad in all black, from his boots to his pointed hat. His face was hidden by a faded brown cloth sack. Straw jutted from his neck and wrists. Dorothy stared at the man's face. Was it all a mask or was it his face? She could not see his eyes as his head turned to the ground below.

"We found him snooping around, probably spying for the witch. He was weak... and his magic was almost useless. He managed to kill three of our party, but we subdued him in the end."

"By the Mighty Hammer!" cried out Brawner. "Could it possibly be? I thought he had died years ago."

"Yes, it is, and he lives—for now. Behold the scareman in all his glory!"

A dwarf kicked him in the back of his skinny legs, and he collapsed to his knees.

The scareman hobbled forward to the two dwarves as spears poked his back. He looked up, his eyes tired and worn. Brawner looked at the scareman, who now stood the same height as he gazed into his dark eyes.

"We will burn you... and roast demon meat over the flames, you bastard."

The scareman just looked at the truck, paying little attention to Brawner's threats. He then looked over to Dorothy as the dwarves helped him to his feet.

"Humph... so strong when you're equipped with your magic... and so weak without. Just an old feeble wizard made of straw, pathetic," Brawner said, as he spat on the ground in disgust.

Dorothy approached the small circle of dwarves with the gun in her hand. Conan lagged playfully behind her.

"We will burn him tonight. A feast, if you will, a celebration of his capture," Orff said with confidence. "For years the land thought he was dead," he said to Dorothy. "But now our revenge will be ever so sweet!"

Brawner grabbed the scareman by his shirt. "No! I demand he die now! He made it rain. He was the reason for the slaughter, the fall of our land. All the deaths of humans and dwarves are on his bloody hands!"

Orff looked at the scareman with a thin smile. "See how much more gracious I am than my mountain brothers?"

"I did not make it rain," the scareman said with a surprising calm in his cadence.

Dorothy looked at the scareman, who locked eyes with her.

"Fine machine," he said in admiration. He smiled, and under the cloth, she caught his curled lips and yellow teeth.

She shuddered for just a second. Was he man or monster or possibly both?

"He does not look like much of a threat. I mean, he is thin, weak, and made of straw!" Dorothy said.

"Young lady, he is the most wanted person in all the land, for his horrible behavior, and for the destruction of our world. He is a wizard, and he's very, very intelligent, but mostly ... very, very evil. He made it rain and threw our world into darkness."

The scareman smiled and gave Dorothy a flirtatious wink.

"Enough talk," Brawner shouted. "Let's burn him!"

The group of dwarves all chanted, "Burn him!" and they dragged his body across the road to a barren field.

Dorothy followed after the dwarves as they speedily tied the scareman to a cross of dead wood. The dwarves kept chanting, "Burn, burn, burn!" Several of the captors began to light small torches.

The scareman twitched. His eyes were wide open as flames danced dangerously close to his strawlike body.

Dorothy looked at the scareman. He reminded her of a painting her aunt had of the crucifix back in the diner. It was gaudy and did not fit in, but her uncle got it in Italy and said it was good luck, and it had been in the back corner of the diner for years. She found it depressing, but her aunt could not let it go.

"Do not feel pity for me, child," the scareman called out to her. "I know you are lost. I also know that only I can return you home."

Dorothy's heart stopped. Could he? What if he really was a wizard? The dwarves chanted louder and louder as they encircled the scareman. Dorothy ran into the midst of the mob.

"Wait... Wait!" she cried out.

The dwarves grumbled and looked at Dorothy angrily. She looked up into the scareman's dark eyes.

"Tell me what you know, and I may be able to save you."

The scareman let out a laugh. "Death is just the escape I want, young lady, but I will tell you, only I can send you back."

"How? How do you know this...?"

"Because, my child, I am the one who brought you here ... to this place. I command the winds and rain... all the elements but fire. I sent my winds to your land. You have been chosen to save this world."

"What? You want me to believe this? Let him burn," Dorothy said as she began to walk away through the mob.

"Well, if I die, you may really never know... will you? Hope you like cloudy days, as you'll never see the sun again here in our world."

The dwarves were getting reckless, and the shouts of burning began once more. Dorothy stopped and considered what he had said. Lie or not, he said he was possibly the only one who could get her home... What if he wasn't lying? Dorothy walked back to the wooden cross and gazed out at the mob.

"Wait! He claims he can send me back to my home!" she shouted.

"He lies!" a dwarf yelled.

"He says he sent for me!"

"Another lie!" another shouted. "He is the greatest of liars!"

Dorothy realized words were nothing in this land. So, she did what any desperate young lady with a handgun would do. She fired into the air. The sound echoed, and the dwarves backed up in a hurry.

"What is that?" Orff asked.

"It's called a Smith & Wesson. It's a weapon of power ... of magic. I need to keep this wizard alive. I know how he harmed you, but he claims he is the only one who can send me home. Please, I have no other options," Dorothy begged.

"Dorothy, he is deceiving you. He will do whatever he can to escape. He is pure evil..."

"I know, but he may be all I have. What if he can get me home?"

"Dorothy... he is a merciless killer. He slew many dwarves and humans and destroyed the army of the Iron Soldiers on the battlefield! He made it rain!"

"Oh, did I, now?" the scareman shouted in his defense. "I was not on the battlefield, and I never brought the rains... I never raised a hand to dwarf or human. I was kept captive by the witch!"

"Don't lie! We know you are the witch's tool, a servant of dark magic..."

"That was true ... many years ago... but I am now of my own will. I already have an unforgivable amount of blood on my hands."

Orff gave a grim look at Brawner. "What do we do? He is wanted for such terrible crimes... yet rumors are he and the witch have gone their own ways. If the girl freed your people, and he can help her... should we not let him go?"

"I do not know... our freedom, and now *his* freedom? Is she worth it?"

The mob was quiet as the wizard returned his eyes to the ground, waiting for the flames to consume him.

Dorothy turned and looked up at him. "If you cross me, I will surely kill you," she said. "I have lost a lot in the last year, and I am not about to lose my only chance of returning to what little I have. So, I tell you now... you better be telling the damn truth."

The scareman grinned. "Oh, I can get you home. There is only one catch—I must have my book of spells from the witch's castle. You help me recover it, and I give my word I will send you back."

"Damn it!" Dorothy said. "I thought you sent for me..."

"No, not really... I sent for anyone that my whirlwind could find. I guess you lucked out. I would have preferred a warrior, a man, but instead, I received a girl with an attitude problem. You will have to do I suppose." He smirked.

Dorothy filled with anger and turned to the dwarves. "Cut him down!" she yelled. "And pass me a torch. He isn't leaving my damn sight."

The dwarves cut the straw wizard down, and grumbling could be heard as the scareman smiled. "Now, my child, the castle is two days on foot, but with your machine, I bet we can be there much sooner."

Orff and Brawner approached Dorothy. "Don't let him fool you. We will accompany you to make sure he keeps his word."

"No, I will be fine. I have Conan, a gun, and matches. If he steps out of line, I will burn him myself."

The scareman smirked once more.

"That is not wise Dorothy. He is a master of deception," said Orff. "We hope your journey is successful. Any trouble and you are to return to us immediately, understand?"

"Yes, I will," Dorothy said as she put the gun to the scareman's sacklike face. "Now, let's go, before I change my mind!"

Dorothy, Conan, and the scareman climbed into the truck and set off as the dwarves waved goodbye.

"We had better send someone to watch over her, brother," said Brawner.

"I agree," Orff replied. "Let's set up a party and track them. We know better than to trust the strawfilled liar. If he lays a hand on the girl... we burn him alive."

# "THE FOREST OF THE DAMNED"

Dorothy didn't trust the scareman and had Conan sit between them. The Rottweiler himself just stared at the new traveler and once in a while looked out the windshield. The silence was bothering Dorothy, so she put in a CD, and heavy metal pumped from the speakers. The guitars wailed, and the drums echoed. The scareman looked at Dorothy as he shook his head and grimaced.

"I do not know what world you came from, but this music is torture!" he shouted.

Dorothy grinned and shrugged her shoulders.

They drove for nearly ten minutes before trees began to appear. Some were dead, while others clung to life amid scattered green and yellow leaves.

"We're getting closer now!" the scareman announced over the blasting stereo.

"What?" Dorothy asked as she turned down the volume.

"I said we're close now to the Forest of the Damned. So, turn off the noise... I don't want to bring any more attention to us. This machine alone is loud as can be."

"It's called a Ford," Dorothy said. "You don't have machines, do you?"

"Well, we had a few machines, and the humans made the Iron Soldiers." The scareman paused for a moment. "Damn technology, I despise it. It was killing this world."

"This world," Dorothy snapped back, "is no more."

"Well, girl, this world was once a rich and luxurious land filled with life until..." The scareman put his head down and then looked out the window.

Dorothy's frustration mounted as she raised her hand. "Until what...?"

The scareman turned his head and looked at Dorothy. "Until the day it rained, and the witch came into power... and then came the Ten Days of Darkness! Are you happy now?"

He turned and then looked back out the window.

"Hey, don't get pissed at me!" shouted Dorothy. "I don't know your world. I just wanna get my ass back to Kansas! Hell, I could be dead for all I know—if I died and was dragged toward hell, this is how I envision it. But seeing I have my dog, and you, I may just have a way out. I can't bring myself to simply surrender to the inevitable though... so I'm going to keep an open mind. You're going to get me home, and that's all there is to it."

"I'm sorry. You're right..."

"Damn straight," Dorothy snapped back. "I don't need this drama. I have enough back home."

"Your world is in trouble?" the scareman asked.

"No," Dorothy replied. "Not my whole world, just my life. It's a long story, and I don't want to bore you with some soppy tale of my problems. You can fix my biggest problem... getting me back home to all my other problems."

"If I get my book, I can send you home and make things right. Well, as right as I can."

"I just want to get home; you can do whatever the hell you want when I'm gone," Dorothy said.

"Look, if we get to the castle, I may be forced to kill. I hope that doesn't offend you—I do not have my book, but I still know several spells... though I'm not as strong as I once was. This straw body has weakened me so much," the scareman said and cleared his throat. "I am not who I once was. Our world has many problems, and so force will be necessary. I just wanted to warn you in advance, you being a girl and all."

Dorothy gritted her teeth, swallowed hard, and looked ahead through the cracked windshield. "Kill all you want. Make it rain blood for all I care. I just wanna get back. I'm a bit numb to all of this, and if it wasn't for all the pain, I wouldn't know quite who I am. I may lose my mind, but I'm numb to it. It'll take a lot of darkness to make me want to stop moving, and I'm not some girl that needs a man to get her through the day. I don't know what kind of women you have in this world, but in mine, we're far from weak."

"I just thought knowing of our world would help and..." began the scareman.

"What don't you get is that all I want is to get back home, sell some tools and this truck, help save my aunt's diner, oh, and cancel my wedding due to a cheating fiancé! I'm still trying to pay off my father's funeral while finishing school. You want to hear more of my problems?"

"No," the scareman replied.

"Good... now we're even," Dorothy answered back.

The scareman let out a chuckle. "You're a lovely girl. This may be fun."

"Don't get comfortable, Stitch-face. I don't need a friend right now. All I need is to get home."

"Good, you won't find a friend in me," he said, crossing his arms and looking back out of the window.

Suddenly Dorothy felt a vibration in her pocket and quickly pulled out her phone.

"I have service?" she asked and looked at the phone.

"Kill the witch, save the world!" her phone blasted.

"Why does that little machine order you to kill the witch?" the scareman asked.

"Ugh, it's just a game on my phone. It does that sometimes. It's a glitch. I need to delete the stupid thing."

"A game on your machine?"

"Yes, my world has a lot of machines and a lot of games. It's nothing."

"I can tell you the witch certainly does not play games," the wizard said.

Dorothy slid her phone back into her pocket. "I just want to go home," she said angrily.

The trees were fuller now, and some even bore fruit while some remained dead and barren. More rolling hills and shrubs passed on the side of the dirt pathway as the truck sputtered along. The gray sky went on for miles.

"Man, this is a weird place," Dorothy noted. "Like Seattle..."

"It was not always this odd, at one time it was beautiful—" The scareman cut himself short. "Just keep moving this machine. I have to try to remember some spells to get us into the castle. The witch's magic is very powerful. She also has a strong general in command of her army of evil—The Necro Lord. He has eyes all over our world, raising the dead using magic most dark. I'm hoping we can avoid him altogether. Maybe we can use this machine or other things from your world against the witch."

"Let me ask you something. If this witch is so evil... why doesn't someone just kill her? I mean, use an arrow, a spear, hell... a big rock would do the job! I mean, killing is simple to you, isn't it? You fought many battles, right? Don't people rise up, rebel, foment? In my world, leaders have been the victims of the mob since the dawn of time," Dorothy said.

"You do not understand, child... she *has* been shot by arrows, poisoned; there have been many attempts on her life. She's been stabbed, beaten, and set alight... but I made an unforgivable mistake... she is unstoppable. She cannot be killed by any element of our world, and it's all my fault. I put a spell on her when I believed she was going to help me destroy the machines once and for all... but she decided to instead simply annihilate all who opposed her."

"Oh... now I see why those dwarves wanted so badly to execute you—this is all your fault," Dorothy said.

"No, well, in some ways, I mean..." the scareman sputtered. "I would rather not discuss this, and if we meet her, I will need all my strength, so please let me concentrate."

"Okay. Just save some strength to send me and my dog back home. That's all I care about right now."

Dorothy slowed the truck down as a glimmer caught her eye. She peered through the cracked windshield, and far in the distance there appeared a massive clearing from the thick trees. Something seemed to shine down through the forest, like a lost sunbeam bouncing off melting snow. It glimmered, shone brightly, and blinded Dorothy for a brief second. She squinted and turned to the scareman.

"What the hell is that?" she asked the scareman. Dorothy looked left through the cracked windshield to see more and slowed down the truck.

"What are you doing? We have to go faster; we cannot waste any time," the scareman ordered.

"Hold on. What is over there? I wanna go look."

Dorothy drove the truck off the dirt road onto a field of dead grass.

"This is not a good idea at all. We need to continue on our way," the scareman said, a hint of fear in his tone.

"I just wanna see," Dorothy said.

"There is nothing to see—now get back on the road!" the scareman said with a strong sense of desperation.

Dorothy slammed on the brakes. "Okay listen. *I'm* driving; *you're* sitting. I have a gun. I've a hair trigger, and your attitude isn't helping. I just wanna see... stay here!"

"Fine. If I knew you would have been such a drama queen, I would have let the dwarves kill me and end my suffering. So be it, go and look. And I do *not* have a bad attitude," the scareman said in retort.

"Whatever, stay in the truck. If you run out on me, I will find you and burn you to death... and I'll take my time doing it; your attitude will be the least of your worries." Dorothy got out of the truck after she removed the keys from the ignition and gave a big fake smile to the scareman.

"Be right back... coward."

Conan leaped out and ran alongside her.

Dorothy walked up the sloping field as the scareman leaned out. "Hurry back... do not waste time! You want to get home, don't you? Well, this is just slowing us down!"

He then sat back and looked out the window into the woods. He felt as if they were being watched.

"Stupid girl! Damn tornado... we needed a man, a warrior, a leader, not her! Stupid, stupid, stupid!"

Dorothy arrived at the top of the hillside and was confronted by a statue nearly ten feet tall. Its body was massive, with huge arms and thick legs, intimidating even though it kneeled with its head down in apparent resignation. It resembled a robot. It had rivets and armor plating all over its hulking form. Its arms were chained to a giant granite slab. Its head resembled a skull-like helmet similar to that of a knight. Thin vines wrapped around the statue like a giant tombstone in an unkempt cemetery. Rust covered several of its joints. In one hand was a fierce-looking battle axe. It had no rust and shone Dorothy's reflection as she looked at it. At the base of the stone was written—"THE MIGHTY ACHILLES... Here is your Savior!"

Dorothy looked at the statue; she felt almost drawn to it. She slowly raised her hand and caressed the head. She glanced around. There were bolts and iron pieces scattered along the grass. She walked around the hulking iron statue and saw other heads and arms scattered about.

"This isn't a statue. It's one of the iron men the dwarves talked about!" Dorothy mumbled. "It was one of their machines."

Conan sniffed around the iron man's feet and began to lift his leg.

"No, bad dog!" Dorothy shouted. Conan tilted his head in disappointment and jumped up on Dorothy.

"Okay, boy, down. Just piss somewhere else."

Conan jumped down, more than satisfied with the compromise.

Dorothy stepped back toward the iron soldier and tore off the vines so as to look closer at the skull-like face. She leaned in and stared into the sockets. "Wow! This is awesome... like something out of a video game."

Suddenly, the eyes flickered, and green light shone, and Dorothy stumbled back with a small scream and fell.

After she regained her composure, she stood up and looked into the face once more.

The eyes were lifeless.

"Damn... that was weird." She looked closely at it again. And suddenly once again, the eyes lit up.

"Oh my God!" Dorothy covered her mouth and whispered in awe. "It still works!"

She sprinted down the hill to her truck, Conan bounding behind her. She ran to the cab of the truck and flung open the door.

"That thing is still working! I saw its eyes... it's one of those Iron Men, right?"

"What!" cried the scareman. "It's working? No, impossible, it's dead; they were all destroyed..." The scareman paused before ordering, "Let's get out of here!"

"No way, you're hiding something—that iron man is definitely something of note. There's a plaque by his feet and everything. He was a war hero, right? Back home we honor our veterans and praise their deeds as a show of respect."

"He is not a hero. He is there as an example to those who dare defy the witch. He has been there for years. We need to go, now!"

"Go? No way! I wanna get him working. He could help us! It's like a walking tank!"

"Oh, I doubt it would work now, and besides, it's all rusted. Trust me, it's nothing more than old, rusted junk. We best not waste what little time we have... Let's just go."

"Wait, I have tools in the back of the truck!" exclaimed Dorothy. "Do they run on electricity or gas or what?"

"What are gas and electricity?" the scareman snorted. "They ran on steam. They burned with concentrated pressurized woods and coal."

"Oh, wow... we had engines like that long before I was born. Steam Engines using coal and wood... That was a long time ago, but I'm still gonna try. I think we can get him runnin'. He has some life in him. I saw it in his eyes! He must have a power source that is still working."

"Dorothy, please, listen to me... even if he is still working you do not want to awaken him, and furthermore, we cannot stay. We're in great danger here, and night is just hours away, so can we please keep going while it is still light?"

Dorothy, however, had already made her way to the back of the truck and opened the toolboxes.

The scareman got out of the truck with a mumble most foul. "She doesn't listen to reason... I would kill her if I thought it would help me."

"Come on!" Dorothy said, and with her hands full of tools, she began to tear up the hillside. The scareman climbed from the truck and followed behind her at a very, very cautious pace. He mumbled and rambled under his breath, still complaining, still furious.

After Dorothy arrived at the statue, had removed all the vines, and took out a spray can, she turned to the scareman. "See this, it's WD-40. It can loosen anything." She took the can and started on the head and neck. She then shook the can, went down the arms, and drenched the hands. The fluid dripped off the Iron Soldier's arms, coating his body.

She returned to the head, sprayed the jaw, and then took both her hands and began to move the jaw slowly. It creaked at first and then began to move with ease. "Wow, this guy sure is rusted."

She then took a wire brush and began to remove the flakes and pieces of rust from his hands and arms.

"Well... I see no lights in his eyes. Can we get the hell out of here now?" the scareman suggested.

"No way! Anyway, you know a lot more than me about these machines. Why won't you help?"

"There is no way I'm helping him. This is a grave mistake and a waste of precious time. I thought you wanted to go home!" the scareman shouted.

Dorothy looked at the Iron Soldier. "Come on. I know you're in there... Just try to move somehow."

The lights in the sockets lit up, there was a small pop, and then they faded.

"He will not work, Dorothy; the witch made sure of it. I refuse to help you with him, and that is final," the scareman said as he crossed his straw arms.

Suddenly the head twitched, and a dull hum began. The green eyes flickered once more.

"Oh, yeah? I think he still has some life in him... like a classic car," Dorothy countered.

Dorothy pulled on the Iron Soldier's arms and, using her body weight, leaned and lifted and rotated the shoulders in small circles.

The light turned off.

"Damn!" Dorothy said. "What do I have to do to get him working?"

The scareman walked over in front of the rusted warrior and looked into his eyes.

"Dorothy, he was put here to live in a tormented state, less death than eternal torture. Do you see the field, the heads, the parts strewn everywhere? This field was the fall of this warrior and his army, the end of the rebellion of machines. The witch put him here and kept him alive with just enough power to see... so every day he opens his eyes and witnesses once more the warriors that fell under his command. He sees the failure and feels the pain of the last battle of a doomed war. He led the humans, a few creatures of magic, dwarves, and the other Iron Soldiers. Don't you see? The witch made an example of him and still sneers over his daily torment. There is nothing we can do here. We need to leave, now."

Dorothy thought of the betrayal of her fiancé. Was this scareman any better than that bastard who used her and threw her away without a care for her at all? Maybe the dwarves were right. She took in a deep breath and cleared her head for a second. "You know a lot about him.

I suppose you were there helping the witch, seeing the rebellion fall, and I bet you helped put him here in this field, didn't you? That's why you are so hated throughout the kingdom."

"I was on the field of battle, but I only watched. I did not place him here—that was after I realized the error of my ways. And yet I still harbor a hatred toward machines. They were the downfall of our world."

"No, you sadistic son of a bitch! Now I get it. *You're* the downfall! You didn't want to try new things, and the whole world suffered for your cowardice. You didn't want to grow and learn! You reviled the renaissance, you're just a power-hungry, feeble little man, and now you're hiding from everything and everybody!" Dorothy said and looked back at the Iron Soldier, before stepping up to the scareman.

Dorothy took out a lighter and held it inches from the scareman.

"What's that?" he asked.

She flicked the lighter, and fire rose. "It's all I need to kill you," she said. "It's not an eternal flame, but it'll do the job."

She then took the can of WD-40 and sprayed it over the lit flame of the lighter.

The scareman fell back and covered his face with his straw arms. "Make it stop! Or I will have no choice but to kill you, you foolish girl!"

Dorothy lifted her finger from the nozzle of the WD-40 and stared at the scareman with flushed, angry cheeks.

"Now listen! Either help me fix him, or I'll kill you right here. I'm beginning to think the dwarves were right... I am foolish, foolish enough to help you. This fallen world is your damn fault. Maybe, just maybe, if we work together, this Iron Soldier can help us both get me home."

The scareman laughed. "I would like to see that! A machine to return you home. Only I can do such magic."

Dorothy raised the lighter once again. "Do you enjoy the magic of my fire?"

The scareman was furious. He stormed back and his glovelike hands twitched. "I could kill you, child! If you ever cast that magic again, I will weave a spell that will tear you in two."

"Good, try it, and I'm sure my dog will tear you apart like a sofa cushion."

"I need my spell book! Damn it!" The scareman turned and walked around in a circle, cursing in a language Dorothy could not understand. It seemed he was on the verge of losing his mind.

The mood was grim as Dorothy put the lighter away. "Look, I need *you* more than you need *me*. I'm well aware of that. I simply want to go home. You need the book. If we work together, we can achieve both goals. I'm sorry... I am lost, confused... whatever my machine and tools from my world can help you get your book back, I will use to help you. Truce?"

The scareman looked at the young woman. "You're right... you *do* need me more," he said arrogantly. "But I need you as well, and I definitely need my damn spell book. I can fix this, I swear. I can fix everything."

The scareman walked up to the Iron Soldier and looked at Achilles's face. "I hate machines," he mumbled. "They have no heart."

Suddenly the two iron arms flew up and snapped the chains from the slab. In one quick sweep, he grabbed the scareman, placing him in a bear hug. Achilles pulled him in tighter and looked at the scareman. His head twitched as the metal groaned and creaked. A thin trail of steam lightly rose from his neck.

The scareman screamed, "He has me! Get him off... I can't throw a spell without the use of my hands!"

Dorothy quickly pulled on the arms, but they didn't move.

"He is crushing me!" the scareman cried.

Achilles then brought him in even closer and glared into the scareman's dark eyes. A low grumbling metallic voice snarled. There came from his mouth nothing that made sense, however. Achilles fought again and tried to speak once more, but only a metal grinding emerged.

Dorothy grabbed the can of WD-40 and sprayed it inside the jaw and mouth of the Iron Soldier.

"Oh, that's great! Now I can hear him yell in triumph as he rips me to straw pieces!" the scareman screamed.

"No, he is trying to ask you something."

The scareman noticed the grip on his arms loosened. He could break free. He looked at the Iron Soldier, hoping it was not a trap.

Achilles tried once more to speak. "Why did you make it rain?" came a metallic whimper.

He then shouted it louder, "Why did you make it rain?!"

The scareman looked blankly ahead.

Achilles shouted again and again, stronger with each metal scream until he tightened his grip on the scareman and finally threw the scareman to the ground.

The scareman scurried over to Dorothy and watched as Achilles sank his head into his hands and screamed out in agony.

"Oh my God, he is really pissed..." Dorothy said and pulled out her gun. "I don't know if even this gun will slow him down."

"I told you we should have not tried to free him. Even my magic is limited against machines—that's why we tried to stop them years ago."

"Well, obviously, he has more heart than you or the witch ever thought."

The Iron Soldier was still rusted in a kneeling position as he looked up at Dorothy. "Please... free my legs. I haven't moved in so very long."

The scareman shook his head as Dorothy stared at the great iron warrior.

"Please, I must set things right for my Iron Soldiers and for my creators. I beg of you... please."

The scareman shook his head even faster, but Dorothy slowly approached the hulking iron warrior.

She was cautious, even standing several feet away from his mighty reach. "I will help you if, and only if, you promise not to harm us. We need your help."

Achilles looked at the scareman. "He will get no help from me... but if you free me, I will be indebted to you, though you keep strange and evil companions, it seems. I will protect you until I can get my revenge on that witch!"

"Okay, that's fine... you have a grudge, that's understandable. Just remember to keep me safe."

The scareman just stood up and shook his head. "Bad idea," he repeated, again and again.

Dorothy took the can of WD-40 and coated the thick iron legs. Achilles tried to move his rusted knees and hips, and pushed and tugged, slowly working the fluid into his joints.

"Oh my! That feels so wonderful!" he groaned. "I haven't seen a human in so long... but they created me, so I will trust you for now, and I will help you. You have my word."

The scareman was now pacing and trying to remember spells. He babbled words and looked nervously at Achilles.

"I am going to try to stand, better get back... I don't want to crush you," Achilles said.

"No problem," Dorothy said, quickly darting over to the scareman.

Achilles groaned and slowly inched his way up. He shook as he rose, and the sound of metal grinding pierced Dorothy's ears as his joints and limbs wobbled and creaked.

The iron warrior then stood tall and reached out his arms toward the gray sky. He then roared and seemed to stretch as steam poured from his neck and joints.

The scareman hid behind Dorothy and mumbled some spell followed by the words, "No, that's not it. Good Lord, he is going to kill me."

Achilles now stood proud. He picked up his axe and, with great effort, walked over to Dorothy. She gazed up at the warrior, who stood nearly twelve feet tall. His massive arms swung like hydraulic jacks. He looked around, raised his axe in victory, and cried with all his might, "Freedom! Sweet freedom!"

"I told you this was a bad idea," the scareman said.

"Listen, young woman..." Achilles began.

"My name is Dorothy," she said with a sweet smile.

"Dorothy, that is a very pretty human name," he said. "I hope your journey is swift, for I have so much to set right, so many things to do, and a witch with whom I plan to settle the score once and for all."

"Oh, we were on our way to her castle right now."

The scareman put his hand over Dorothy's mouth, but it was too late.

"Her castle... Do you work for her as well?" Achilles asked. Steam shot from his neck. "Is this deceiving wizard taking you there to imprison you?"

"No, listen... I'm not from this world, and I can't get home. The scareman told me he has a book of spells, and if I help him retrieve the book, he can send me back."

"And you believe him?" sneered Achilles. "The great deceiver?"

"I don't have a choice," replied Dorothy. "I met with some dwarves, and they told me all about the scareman. When I saved him from a fiery execution, he said he would help me get home. I'm begging you to no longer think of him as an evil wizard... just an old soul, and a harmless one at that."

"The dwarves were wise to warn you of this traitor. He speaks nothing but lies. He caused the fall of our world; he made it rain. He was the architect of the Seven Days of Darkness."

"I did not cause the rain!" the scareman shouted. "I never caused the rain! First, it was Two Days of Darkness; then I heard Three Days of Darkness... Now it's Seven Days of Darkness. You people are all rumor-spreading parasites!"

Achilles stepped up and confronted the wizard. "You lie and use people. I will not let you use anyone anymore. I will go with the girl and kill the witch myself, and if you cannot send her back... I will destroy you myself."

"*I* will send her back *if* we get my spell book. As for the rain, I swear I never sent it... the witch stole the pages from my spell book! After she cast the spell, there was no way of reversing it. *She* made it rain, you iron-headed lunk!" the scareman shouted.

"Hate to break up this stroll down dreary lane," Dorothy said, "but we can all agree we have much to do, so we better move—and I don't know about you, but I'm getting hungry."

The scareman looked around. "There are several trees around that bear good fruit. I will go and gather some." He then stormed off.

Achilles looked down at the truck. "I'll let you know if he brings you poisonous fruit. We are created to aid humans, not like him." He glanced again at the truck yards away. "What kind of machine is that?"

"Oh, it's a Ford F350 Club Cab... Wanna check it out?"

"Yes, I would," he paused, "um, like to check it out."

Dorothy and Achilles walked down to the truck. The ground shook just a little with every step from the iron warrior.

"He isn't all that bad, ya know," Dorothy said.

"No, he is pure evil... he is simply powerless without his book of spells. He is afraid of the witch, which means he must be desperate to be returning to her domain. I am curious, however, why he left her and is now among us. Don't worry though, Dorothy, I am here to protect you, and I will serve you until my last breath."

Dorothy blushed and smiled. "Wow, thanks."

The two new allies arrived at the truck and waited for the scareman to return with dinner.

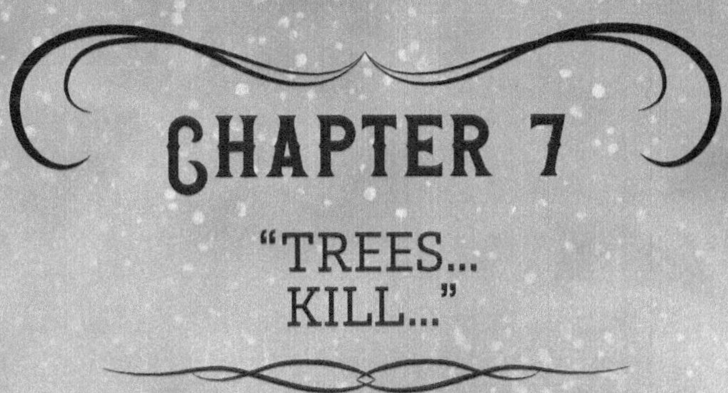


## "TREES...
## KILL..."

After the scareman returned with some freshly picked fruit and Dorothy had eaten what looked like a pear but tasted like an orange, the three adventurers began to relax. Dorothy plugged her phone into the cigarette lighter to charge it. Achilles watched the road and stood guard while Dorothy scrambled around in the cab of the truck. She dug around and found some old CDs, a bag of beef jerky, and a box of shotgun shells behind the seat. There were also a couple of bottles of water and a few magazines with girls on the covers, wearing bikinis and holding wrenches.

The scareman pouted as he walked over a small hill, found an area of dead yellowing grass, and lay down. He leaned his head against a tree and folded his hands on his chest. He watched Dorothy scramble.

"Stupid girl... I cannot believe we have to take that iron, clunky, beastly machine with us—no matter, I guess, I can always dispose of him when I retrieve my book."

Without warning, the tree rustled and groaned. The scareman looked up as a face appeared in the deep bark.

"So Scareman, you want your precious book back?" asked the tree.

"What? I thought you were just a tree, not one of the witch's servants!" the startled scareman replied.

"Oh, I am more than a tree. Word travels fast... and if I bring you and the girl to the witch, I am sure of a magnificent reward. I need simply to kill Achilles and take you and the girl back to our dark queen," the tree hissed.

Its roots ripped from the soil, and its branchlike arms tightened.

The scareman jumped to his feet. "Well, you better have a better plan than that, as my magic will easily crush you!"

The tree let out a laugh. "Come now. You are weak and feeble. You have no spells without your book. Everyone in the land knows of your fall from power, and her manipulating you all along. Maybe you're not the smartest in the land..." The tree let out a chuckle.

"I have enough strength remaining to take care of the likes of you!" the scareman shouted.

Just then, several of the dead trees nearby joined in the laughter. The scareman looked around as close to half a dozen trees uprooted and encircled him.

"Your move, Strawman..." the thick tree said.

"Hey now, wait a second, I'm warning you..." the scareman sputtered.

The lead tree reached down with his branchlike arm and swatted the scareman back to the dead grass. Though he was shaken and some of his straw had fallen from his boots and gloves, the scareman leaped to his feet, raised his hands, and gritted his teeth... then suddenly took off and fled back over the hill and raced down to the truck.

Achilles spotted him first.

"Oh no, looks like trouble," Achilles said as he grabbed his axe.

"Something has him spooked... Maybe he *is* powerless without his book," Dorothy replied.

The scareman ran straight to Achilles and looked up at him. "How do you feel, my great iron friend? The Mighty Achilles is always ready for battle, yes?" he asked, panting.

"Friend? Oh, I think not, Scareman. However, I have not met a foe in battle for so long... back away from me, Scareman," Achilles ordered.

The scareman patted Achilles's hulking iron arm.

"Well, that is just what we need, as we have company," the scareman said before stepping over to Dorothy.

Achilles and Dorothy glanced to the hill as slowly the demonic trees appeared, their branchlike arms swaying wildly.

"What the hell are those things?" Dorothy asked.

"Humph. The witch's little imps," Achilles said. "Looks like I get to cut me some firewood."

"Dorothy, do you have any more fire? We can only burn them with fire. It's the only thing they fear," the scareman said.

"Yes. We can make fire," Dorothy said.

"I'll give them something to fear!" Achilles shouted.

He then stepped forward to protect Dorothy and the scareman.

"I'll cut them down, and you two stack the bodies!" he ordered.

Achilles then turned and started marching toward the enemy, the earth shaking under each heavy step that sank into the soft soil.

"Listen, Dorothy, get us some fire. We need to scare them, or burn them, whatever it takes—they are nearly impossible to kill without fire no matter what that iron clod intends. They are dead, like rotting timber, so they burn quickly. Fire is our only chance. He cannot beat that many by himself!" the scareman said nervously.

"Okay, hold on," Dorothy said as reached into her pocket. Her hand emerged empty, however. "It must have fallen out of my pocket in the truck!" she said as she scurried into the cab and searched in desperation.

The scareman looked on nervously as Achilles began shouting taunts of his power and exploits.

"Come on, you seedless hell spawns!" he shouted.

The demon trees quickened their pace as Achilles grinned and raised his axe. Rusty or not, his anger fueled his internal furnace, and steam puffed from his neck. He was back and ready to cut timber.

Dorothy crawled out of the truck and pulled out a gas can, a hunting bow, and several rags.

"I think we can use this stuff..." she said as she began to pour the gas on the rags.

"Can't you do any magic, Scareman? I mean, come on, you have been bragging for hours, and now you're hiding behind me..."

"I cannot do fire. My straw won't create fire. I can do all elements, but fire... but I cannot remember my spells. It's simply been so long, and my memory has faded since the witch turned me to straw. It may be hard to believe, but there was a time I was the most intelligent man in all the land."

Dorothy began to tie the gas-covered rags to the arrows. "Sounds like a piece of ass wiped your brain... I'm assuming that's what happens to most men, no matter how smart they are."

The scareman nodded his head. "Yes, well... That and lies and good intentions."

"No surprise there... Well, you better start remembering quickly 'cause I'm not that good with a bow and my guns won't do anything to walking trees."

Achilles now squared off and stood just a few meters from the approaching enemy.

The head tree growled. "So, Achilles, it appears you are free. We thought about taking you alive again, but after we talked it over, we decided we would simply kill you ourselves."

"Well, you fruitless saplings... come show me how weak is your bark!" he thundered back.

The trees charged, and Achilles ran to meet them in battle. With a war cry, he swung his axe at the roots of the first assailant, who cried out and fell to the ground. Achilles then raised the axe once more and struck him in the back repeatedly. Several of the trees grabbed at him. He quickly ducked, however, and rolled to the side.

Dorothy was getting her bow ready and lit the gas-soaked tip of the arrow with her lighter. The scareman backed away in fear. Dorothy pulled back and fired, but the arrow missed its mark and landed several feet from the trees. They did take notice, however, and stepped back briefly.

"They have fire over there and another machine!" one of the trees screeched.

"Nice shot," the scareman remarked sarcastically.

"Screw you... I told you I can't fire this thing—I haven't gone bow hunting since my dad died. Why don't you go hide or something? You can't cast spells or be around fire. At least you can stay out of harm's way."

The arrow Dorothy shot was close enough for three of the trees to take notice, and they turned their attention toward the scareman and Dorothy. They scurried with their roots kicking up dirt and dying grass to meet the amateur archer and her cowardly straw companion.

"Oh man, this is not good," Dorothy gasped. "They move quickly."

She lit another arrow. The scareman watched Achilles as he leaped from the back of a fallen tree and slammed his axe into another. He moved with a speed and agility remarkable for a hulking iron machine and was surely a sight to behold.

Dorothy pulled back and fired again. This time, the arrow landed a few feet short of the oncoming trees, however. The trees stopped and looked at the fire as one tree took its roots and scraped dirt over the arrow, snuffing out the flame.

"Damn, I can't do this... I can't concentrate, and the bow is way too tight!" Dorothy said in despair.

"Wait! Give me a second; I think I have remembered a spell!" said the scareman.

"You better have, or we're all dead meat!" Dorothy said, and she lit another arrow as the scareman began to mumble. She looked at him and then looked back at the attackers. "Better hurry, Scareman!" she said as she pulled back on the bow. Suddenly the bow loosened, and she pulled it back farther. "What the hell?" she asked.

The scareman stopped mumbling and looked at Dorothy. "Quick! Take them out!"

Dorothy focused and fired the flaming arrow. It sailed through the air and landed in the center of a tree. Sparks and flame began to spread from the gasoline-soaked arrowhead as the tree cried out and ran to the left and then to the right as the fire trailed up its body. It screamed in agony and fell to the ground, trying to put itself out with its branchlike hands.

The other two trees didn't slow down and instead advanced ever quicker.

Achilles turned his head as he heard the dying tree's screams, and a thick branch slammed across his chest, knocking him to the yellow grass.

As Dorothy and the scareman retreated, Dorothy grabbed the handful of rag-tipped arrows and her lighter and quickly ran with the scareman; Conan ran behind her.

There was no time, and they ran from the truck as the two remaining advancing trees charged.

Achilles felt branches on his feet as the remaining trees picked him up off the ground.

Dorothy and the scareman were now several yards away and turned to watch as the two trees began to destroy the truck. They started with the windows and then overturned the truck. Conan ran around them barking, trying to get them to flee from the truck, but they continued their assault.

Dorothy pulled out another arrow. "Damn it, our ride... Now we're totally screwed!" She looked across the dirt and gravel road as Achilles struggled. She handed the scareman the lighter.

"Here I'll pull the arrows back. You light the tips, and I'll fire them! We have to help Achilles!"

"B-b-but..." the Strawman stuttered. "It's fire! And I don't even know how to activate this machine!"

"Just use your thumb and pull this lever down!" shouted Dorothy as she pulled back the arrow, and the scareman held the lighter away from his body and attempted to light the arrow.

"You have to quit shaking! Just light the damn thing before Achilles gets ripped to pieces!" Dorothy yelled.

Suddenly the scareman flicked the wheel, and the flame shot up, lighting the gas-soaked rag. He then dropped the lighter and shook his hand in fear. Dorothy took aim as the trees now began to pummel Achilles, who fought back bravely but in vain.

"Get that thing ready to go!" Dorothy said as she fired the arrow.

It sailed over the two advancing trees and struck one of Achilles's attackers in its side.

The tree screamed and started to run as it caught on fire. Achilles now raised his arm as steam flew from his neck and small thin blades shot out from his forearm. They struck the trees, who backed off and gave him just enough time to stagger to his feet.

The scareman, still shaking, lit another arrow, and Dorothy launched it into the air. It flew true and stuck into the root of another tree, who began to burn.

The two trees by the truck saw their comrades fall and decided to charge Dorothy and the scareman before it was too late. They pushed the truck out of the way and began their advance. Achilles scrambled and raised his axe from the dirt. He ripped it from the ground as the remaining tree approached him. Achilles's iron jaw seemed to smile, and in one fluid motion, he spun and slammed Sun Seeker into the demon tree. The tree howled and toppled over as Achilles beat it with his iron-spiked forearm, bark flying into the air.

Dorothy found out how quickly the trees could move, as the two advancing trees were nearly on top of her. Conan barked wildly at the trees, who seemed simply annoyed with the dog's noise as he ran to and fro, trying to slow them down and protect his master. The scareman became overcome with nerves and fumbled the lighter, which fell to the ground. "Damn!" he said.

Dorothy had no choice and fired the arrow, anyway. It struck one of the trees, who fell back in its attack.

The scareman tried to find the lighter in the grass but failed to as the advancing tree overcame both Dorothy and the scareman. It knocked Dorothy to the ground and then picked up the scareman in its long branch hands.

"You will die now, Scareman!" it screamed.

He began to crush the scareman, who let out a groan, but then suddenly turned furious. He looked at the tree and began to mumble. The tree tightened his grip and the more he tightened, the louder the words from the scareman became. He raised his arms, breaking free as he screamed a chant.

The tree began to shake, and as it did, it dropped the scareman and stood very still. The scareman quickly got to his feet, dusted off his shirt, and made his way to Dorothy as the tree suddenly split down the middle. The tree screamed horribly as its insides tore from through its bark, and as its roots turned black and sap sprayed from its eyes and mouth. It collapsed and shook, twitching in agony.

Dorothy watched as the tree died. "Okay, I have to admit that was both horrible and awesome at the same time."

"I just remembered it! The spell of reversal—it makes things implode!" the scareman said, smiling with pride.

"I may need to be nicer to you," Dorothy noted wryly.

Without warning, a branch came crashing down however and tossed the scareman several yards away. Dorothy looked as the last tree with the arrow lodged in its face was just feet from her and reached out with its branchlike hands. It seemed there was no escape until suddenly there was a giant cracking noise! The tree's face went blank, and it toppled to the ground. Dorothy watched as the great axe found its mark in the beast. Achilles ripped it out and stood over the tree.

"Not bad for an old, rusted Iron Warrior," he said.

Dorothy wiped the sweat from her forehead. "That was way too close..."

Achilles helped Dorothy to her feet. There was a moan as the two looked over at the scareman who lay face down in the dirt.

"We better help him up as well," Achilles said. "Though I would prefer to leave him be."

"I know you would, but I have to get home, and he promises to send me there," Dorothy replied.

"I know, but I still do not trust him."

Achilles walked over, grabbed the scareman by the back of the shirt, and lifted him to his feet.

"Get up, Scareman. We have no time for your napping."

The scareman looked around. "Oh, it's you, the one created to lead us—oh Achilles Swift Axe, savior of our lost world!" he said sarcastically.

The huge iron warrior then gave him a short but strong shove. "Let's go, Dorothy. Unlike this coward, I think your machine needs us," Achilles bellowed.

Dorothy took the scareman's arm and helped him walk down to the truck. Achilles walked several paces in front, refusing to look over his shoulder at the scareman or the girl who appeared loyal to the great deceiver.

"No sense of humor with machines. I bet he blames me for the trees' attack," the scareman told Dorothy. "I didn't do it, and I never made it rain," he said weakly.

"Well, being a wiseass will not win you any friends, and I just want to go home." Dorothy looked at the Ford truck—the dents, the shattered glass. She shook her head, and her eyes watered.

Her head sank.

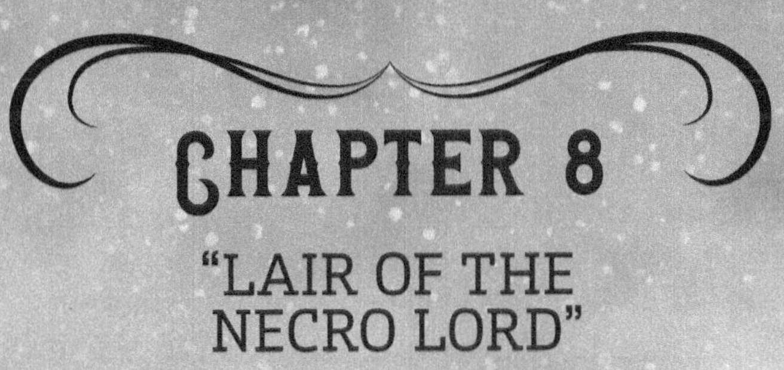

# CHAPTER 8

## "LAIR OF THE NECRO LORD"

The cave was enormous. There were symbols and etchings on the outside of the entrance, and fastened torches brought light to the beginning of the gaping darkness. Voices echoed from inside. Suddenly the voices stopped, and near the cave, four winged creatures with apelike heads and jagged tusks landed.

In their clawlike hands, they held small children. Some were sleeping, others fought, but the struggle was in vain. One of the creatures let out a small guttural bark as the others took the children deep inside the cave. They walked past the witch without even acknowledging her. The witch let out a sigh before following them inside.

In the throne room of the lair, the witch stood close to her resurrected bodyguards. She hated this place—the lair of the Necro Lord. Even with her power, she tried to spend as little time as she could here, but the truth was she needed him more than ever since the scareman left her years ago. It was not that the cave was cold or evil, the witch herself was cold and evil. The Black Mountain, however, was replete with uncontrolled magic and pure chaos. It was as if the caves were alive and there was no control, even with the aid of magic. You could not control things around you perfectly—one spell may work, and yet another may produce a cluster of flowers rather than a vial of poison.

It was a no man's land of magic, death, life, and the unknown, but also a great source of power for those with an affinity for magic and had been for eons—and thus for some, it was worth the risk. The witch herself and her three sisters had visited this place as children centuries ago, and none of them wished to ever go back.

The Necro Lord had found great power here and decided it would be best to make it his place of study and power. As machines took over and magic faded, fewer humans dared go near, and it became more of a myth of a place of magic these last hundred years. It was perfect for the Necro Lord who wished to study and be left alone, if need be, and gain power even with its possible unpredictability.

The Necro Lord sat on a wide stone throne. It was made of black rock; bright red gems trimmed the thick armrests. The light in the lair was bright from the many torches hung from the walls, and gems and gold were scattered about. No one would ever come here to steal from him. The Necro Lord stood up from his seat. His face was hidden behind an oversized hood. His robes were black and tattered. His bony hand took a wooden staff that leaned against his throne.

"Do you really trust your guards with this information?" he asked the witch.

"Why would I doubt them? I saw them; I saw the machine. It was not from our lands. You need to help me learn all you can, or we both may be in great danger. We finally seize power, and now, just a few years later, it is ours to lose? I do not plan on such things."

"You're so cautious. I, however, do not fear anything," he boasted. "I am death. What harm can defeat death?"

"You're a poopie head! We hate you!" a voice echoed from afar.

The Necro Lord pointed his staff into a tunnel. "Be gone! All of you!" He then flew across the room, and the sound of children screaming and running echoed throughout the cave. He turned back to the witch.

"My power only grows. Trust me, we have nothing to fear."

"You seem to fear these haunted caves," the witch said. "The spirits of the dead are restless here."

"Just a bothersome aspect of my magic. I can take the children's essence, but their souls are damned here forever. They think it is all a fun game. I underestimated how this location would hold their souls... especially those of the innocent," he murmured.

"You can always come and dwell in the castle," the witch suggested. "We could build you a cave, a lair... We have an excess of slaves that could use a task to occupy their minds."

"My magic is strongest here in the side of the Black Mountain. In some ways, maybe I am as damned as the children I harvest..."

The witch let out a sigh and looked around.

"You're an evil, stupid head!" echoed a voice in brave defiance.

"Enough! Be gone!" the Necro Lord screamed as he swung his staff, and red light shot into a nearby cave, and once again the children's ghosts fled.

"They only do this when I have company. They ignore me most of the time unless I am ... retrieving essence; then they slow my work."

The four winged creatures stepped into the throne room.

"My Lord, we have returned," the leader grunted.

"Excellent. Take them to the cages," the Necro Lord commanded.

The creatures marched past the witch and disappeared into one of the caves.

"The visitor to our land. We must find her. I will use what I can from the book, maybe a form of magic to locate her, perhaps," the witch suggested.

"I will send my creatures when they are done securing the children. We will find this girl and this machine. I am not worried. Has there been any sighting of the scareman—maybe in a field somewhere scaring away crows?"

"You still hate him after all this time. No, he is still in hiding. As long as I have his book, he is no danger to us," replied the witch.

"That book is more powerful than any of us," the Necro Lord considered. "I'm glad you stole it from him before he learned more of its spells."

"There are spells I still cannot unlock or read. I know he could... but he has deserted us," said the witch.

The witch listened and could hear several children playing in one of the tunnels.

"You really should consider leaving this place. The children's ghosts would drive me mad..."

"Maybe after we learn more of the book's magic, I will leave this place, but for now, I will remain. My magic is stronger here for now."

The witch turned and began to leave. "Keep me informed of any further discoveries. We do not want to give hope to anyone in the Diamond City or even the Ruby City. Such things only result in the torrid stench of rebellion."

"That was crushed long ago, my queen," the Necro Lord said.

The witch smirked and continued to walk from the lair.

The Necro Lord walked back to his throne. He sat down and turned toward a large bookshelf made of stone. Dozens of books coated in cobwebs and dust stared back at him.

"You're a doody head!" a little boy shouted.

The Necro Lord pointed his hand to the voice, and a little boy stood smirking.

"You're a doody head with a carrot nose!"

"Angus, why do you and the others bother me? There are so many caves to play in," the Necro Lord asked.

"Because it's fun! Plus, you cannot hurt us anymore... doody head."

From behind the boy, the four creatures emerged from the darkness and walked through him.

"They are secured, my Lord," the lead creature grunted.

"Good. Now, I have another job for you. It seems we have an unwanted visitor in our land. See if you and the others can find her and her infernal machine."

The creature bowed. "Yes, my Lord." He and the others flew from the lair.

The Necro Lord walked over to the boy and kneeled down. His clawlike hand moved through the ghost.

"Stop! Do not grab at me again," Angus shouted and swung in defiance. His little ghost fists simply passed through the wizard, however.

The Necro Lord laughed. "It's true I cannot hurt you again. But you cannot touch me, boy, for you are dead, and I am alive."

Angus ran, then stopped and looked back. "You're stupid, and we hate you! We want to go home!"

"That will never happen, boy."

"Someday... someday we will get you and go home."

"Not as long as I am alive, and my power is strong in this mountainside," replied the Necro Lord.

"Rip and tear!" Angus shouted. "We will rip and tear and destroy you once and for all!" the boy screamed as he fled into the darkness.

The Necro Lord stood up and slowly walked to the bookshelf, removed a thick book, blew the dust off, and returned to his throne.

# "ATTITUDE IS EVERYTHING"

Dorothy looked at the heap of twisted metal that was once her fiancé's truck. It was flipped, dented like a semi had struck it repeatedly, and she could see many different fluids dripping from under the hood. She walked around it and shook her head in disbelief. "Even if I get back, I can't sell this thing."

"Do you want me to put it back on its proper side?" Achilles asked.

"Can you turn it back over?" Dorothy asked.

"Well, I can try."

The iron warrior bent down and grabbed hold of the side of the truck, and steam flew from his joints as he slowly lifted the vehicle to its side. He gave a mighty push, and the truck came smashing down on its four tires.

"I am sorry about your wonderful machine," Achilles said. "Did it have a name?"

"Um, yeah... Ford."

"Ford, what an odd name," the iron warrior said.

"That was the name of its creator."

The scareman yawned and sighed and looked at Dorothy. "We should probably get moving." He walked to the driver's side door and hopped in.

"Are you nuts? This thing isn't going to run, and if it does, it won't for long," said Dorothy in despair. "See that green mess? That's called antifreeze, and it keeps the engine cool. If it's leaking, that means we have a big problem."

The scareman looked from the passenger side door at the small trail of neon green that dripped.

"Oh, so this machine is broken then."

"Yep, and I do not know if I can fix it," Dorothy said.

"See, that's why I hate machines," said the scareman. "If they break down, what good are they?"

"Well, they help in a lot of situations," Dorothy said angrily. "You don't put all your faith in them to do everything for you; you just hope they help you as best as they can. Machines break down..." Dorothy's eyes began to water. "People break down." Her voice cracked.

"You can put faith in me, Dorothy," Achilles said.

"I bet I can." She wiped her eyes and kicked the tire. She was lost and now stuck. She started to walk away.

The scareman got out of the truck and looked down the dirt trail that led into the forest. "We better get moving. We need to get out of this forest before nightfall. The remains of the Diamond City are a few hours away. If we can get there in time, we may find shelter for the night."

"I agree," Achilles said. "Let's march on."

Dorothy kept walking away.

Her head was down. Conan ran over and tried to console her, but she pushed him down. She stopped and looked around at the dead world. The gray sky stretched as far as she could see.

Achilles began to walk to Dorothy, but the scareman raised his hand and stopped him.

"She is not like you; she is human… Give her a minute."

"She is strong, though. I will fetch her back."

"No, we humans need to … have moments."

"I do not understand," said Achilles.

"I know. Just watch and wait."

Dorothy cried and then screamed. It echoed across the fields. She wiped her eyes, turned, and stormed back toward the truck.

"She is strong, for a girl," the scareman mumbled under his breath.

Dorothy walked back to the truck and looked at the scareman. "Okay, let's go get that damn book, so you can get me home, right?" she asked.

"Yes," he said.

"We may have lost our vehicle, but we can still use some of the things inside. Maybe I can find some stuff we can use on our little horrible adventure."

Dorothy crawled into the cab of the truck and pulled out her school backpack. She emptied the bulky school-books out and walked to the back of the truck. "Won't need these if we have to find a book, fight a witch, and kill resurrected warriors or demon trees. Hey, Stitch-face, come on and help me."

She then got into the back of the truck and raised the cab door. All of the tools and coffee cups were strewn about as Dorothy began to dig around. She took out several more arrows and handed them to the scareman and removed some rope. She then crawled into the back seat of the cab.

She found Bob's shotgun, to her great relief. She then took handfuls of shells and began putting them in her backpack. "Rednecks," she said, smiling to herself. "We're ready for anything, even your shitty lost world.

Bob was always paranoid about running out of gas with nothing to eat 'til help arrived... I bet I find some food in here somewhere."

"What are those you're putting in your pack?" the scareman asked.

"They're shells for this gun... the little gun takes different bullets than this bigger gun."

"So, the bigger gun is better?"

"Um, well, it depends on your target. Shotguns can create a huge mess if fired close, like sending dozens of small metal balls through your body."

"I need no gun, just Sun Seeker will do," Achilles said confidently and lifted the mighty axe.

"Could I see one of those shells?" the scareman asked. Dorothy handed him a yellow shell and then crawled out from the back of the truck bed. The scareman sniffed the shell and looked puzzled.

"I can smell deep odor, but cannot place it."

"That would be gunpowder," Dorothy said.

"We have no such thing here in our world, and I know of all elements from our world—even from the shores of the Realm of the Lion. I bet you this element could kill the witch!" he said happily. "This is definitely an element not of our world."

"With a shotgun, you can kill most anything. Maybe we should just find her, shoot her, and then find your book?"

"It would never be that simple," replied the scareman. "We will have to devise a plan. The witch is no fool, and she is surely well aware you're here. She will try to find you," the scareman said. "If this weapon and this gunpowder can kill her, then let me carry it. I wish to kill the witch myself."

Achilles let out a laugh. "*You* kill the witch! I do not see that happening. Besides, I will strike her down before you point that strange weapon at her or remember a spell."

"We will see, Machine. I don't break down like Dorothy's Ford," the scareman said.

"No, but you forget like an old human," Achilles countered.

"If I had my book, I could rust you from head to toe in an instant!" the scareman boasted.

Achilles just laughed.

"Come on, boys, we don't have time for this," Dorothy said as she slung the backpack over her shoulder. She looked around near the floorboards, and, to her delight, her phone was still attached to the charger.

"Well, finally something is going our way." She took her phone and looked at the power. The phone was at 79%. She picked up the shotgun and began to walk away from the truck.

"Dorothy?" Achilles asked, "What is that tool?" Achilles pointed to the back of the dented truck where one of the side toolboxes had popped open. A long-jagged bar stuck out.

Dorothy walked around to the back of the truck, examining the dented and ruined truck bed and toolbox. "Oh, that's a chainsaw, but it's way too big and heavy. I can't even get it started... I tried once and really messed up my shoulder. Bob uses it to clear out shrubs and trees."

"Trees?" Achilles asked.

Dorothy smiled at Achilles and, without a second thought, climbed into the back of the truck and pulled the giant chainsaw from the open toolbox.

"I can't use this. But I bet you could Achilles," she said as she placed it in his thick iron hands.

"You have to yank on this cord, and then it starts up. It's very tight, but I'm sure you can manage it. See these metal teeth? They move really fast and cut things."

Achilles looked very amused. "This is an amazing small machine. So, I pull this cord, and then what?"

"Oh, then you pull on this trigger right here, and it makes the teeth spin. It's very simple, but very powerful and destructive."

"I will try it," Achilles said.

Achilles pulled back on the cord, and the motor roared to life. Smoke poured into the air. He raised it above his head and walked toward one of the dead trees. He looked at Dorothy and the scareman, gave a metal smile, and pulled the trigger as the blade spun to life. He swung down against the tree. The chainsaw pushed back, and splinters of wood and sawdust flew everywhere.

"No!" Dorothy yelled and ran over. "You don't swing it... You let it do the work."

She took Achilles's hands and slowly showed him how to use the chainsaw.

"You see? You let the blades grind down into the tree bark," she shouted over the roar of the engine.

"This is incredible!" Achilles shouted over the chainsaw's buzz.

The scareman refused to be impressed. "It's loud and makes horrible smoke!" he shouted. "Foolish machine... fire kills trees just as well."

Dorothy pressed a button on the chainsaw, and the engine sputtered and stopped. Achilles let out a sigh.

"I know, big guy," Dorothy said. "Playing is fun, but we have to get moving."

Achilles looked sad. "Oh, I am very keen to practice."

"Later, okay? Plus, I need to check the gas in it, and oil the chain. It'll break if we don't take care of it."

"Well, we don't want that to happen," Achilles said loudly. "I love this thing, the mighty chainsaw!"

Dorothy and the iron warrior walked back to the truck. Dorothy looked inside and grabbed two small containers they'd need if the chainsaw was going to continue to be of use to them.

"Bob always was prepared for work; too bad he didn't like to work. He spent all his money on this truck and his tools. I don't even know how we were going to pay for the wedding. He probably wanted to go to Vegas... cheap, lazy bastard," she muttered as she oiled the chain and filled the chainsaw with fuel. "I wish we could take this fuel and other junk with us, but we don't have the room. "

Achilles opened a panel on his huge iron thigh. "I can take the fuel for the chainsaw and the other tools if they are too heavy for your pack."

"Great! Let's load you up."

The scareman looked in the back of the truck. "Any goodies for me in there?"

"I thought you didn't like machines?" Dorothy replied.

"Well... I don't. I just thought maybe you had something I could use."

"I'm sorry we have no magic in our world. We have magicians, but it's not the same."

"That figures, I summoned a girl from a world without magic. Fine, let's just get going. Time is not our friend in these woods." The scareman began to walk off angrily.

"He is so bitter and switches moods so fast... even I have a hard time dealing with him, and I usually get on with anyone that's even a little cool," Dorothy said to Achilles.

"Cool?" he asked. "Are you cold?"

"Oh, sorry. It means relaxed, fun to be around."

"Ah yes, my creators were cool... but this scareman, throwing our world into misery, being despised by all, and now all alone. It's sad, I guess, but he chose his destiny. I doubt he could ever be cool."

Dorothy smiled and dug around the truck for something to give the scareman. She looked at her schoolbooks and grinned. "Hey, Scareman, here is a book of our magic."

The scareman turned around immediately and walked back to the truck. Dorothy handed him a book of elements and one of mathematics.

"Interesting..." he said and began to flip through the pages.

Dorothy then found a hunting magazine and handed it to him. "If you get bored, this one has pictures of curvy women in bikinis."

He took the magazine and stared at the cover of two women in American flag t-shirts and cutoffs, holding knives and guns.

"Do all women in your world fight and hunt?" he asked.

"Only the great ones," Dorothy said, smiling. "Come on, let's go get that book and get me and Conan home."

The three adventurers walked down the dirt road, deeper into the Forest of the Damned. Conan ran ahead, sniffing out trouble and marking his territory on trees and shrubs.

# CHAPTER 10

## "HAIL TO THE KING, BABY"

The gray sky seemed almost as if it was disappearing into darkness as they walked deeper into the Forest of the Damned. The trees were densely clustered together, and strange sounds seemed to surround them. Conan now walked closely next to Dorothy as Achilles walked out in front. Dorothy saw the dirt path end as red bricks embedded in the soil appeared, like cobblestones in an old city back in her world.

"Are we getting closer to her castle?" she asked. "We seem to have found a road."

"Yes, we are getting closer. The bricks of blood spread out from the Diamond city. I'm sure they stopped building here due to the evil nature of this forest," the scareman noted. "We're now on the bloody brick road. The witch painted the bricks with the blood of her enemies, a morbid reminder of who rules our world."

"Blood to color the bricks? Is she really this horrific?" Dorothy asked.

"Dorothy, there has never been anyone more wicked. Pray she does not get her hands on you, for she is little else but pure evil," the scareman said. "She surrounds herself with foul magic and horrible beasts."

"More evil than you?" Dorothy asked with a grin.

"Bah, I am not evil—maybe greedy, power hungry, a bit controlling perhaps, but not evil," he said with a smirk.

"Oh, we have a name for those kinds of people in my world. You're not evil, just an asshole."

"Then fine, I'm an asshole. I was just trying to make things better for everyone," the scareman acquiesced.

"My world has a lot of that thinking, too," replied Dorothy. "People passing laws and demanding others live how they feel is best. They're called politicians... and they're all assholes, too. You could definitely be one of those in my world."

"He is not an asshole. He is a liar. That's worse, I believe..." Achilles stated.

Dorothy let out a long yawn. She stopped and pulled an energy drink from her backpack. "I'm exhausted. Time for a break." She popped the lid and took several sips.

"We should be out of these cursed woods shortly," Achilles said. "Maybe we will find some shelter and rest in the shadows of the Diamond City."

"The quicker the better," the scareman noted. "I have not been in these woods for some time and do not wish to see the horrors within."

Dorothy held her shotgun closer, and her eyes spied shadows that seemed to move. She pulled a small flashlight from her backpack and turned it on. The small beam of light shone across the blood-red colored bricks.

"Did I tell you guys how I hate the dark?" she asked.

"There is nothing to fear in the dark. It's light you have to fear," the scareman said with a laugh.

"Do not frighten her. We both know what evils the witch has in this forest... just keep watch and be on guard."

"We need more light. I have a larger torch," Dorothy suggested.

"No, it would only bring attention to us. If the witch has her flying creatures, they will surely attack," Achilles said. "I do not trust any of these trees, either. Evil surely surrounds us."

Dorothy looked up and saw a break in the trees, revealing the dark sky. She then looked at her cell phone. She glanced at the battery power first; it was at 71%. "We have been walking for nearly three hours... Is this city much farther?"

"Just a bit more," Achilles said. "We may not be able to enter, but I believe we will manage to find refuge on the perimeter. The witch has let her guard down slightly with only one small city left. Also, we would bring a lot of unwanted attention if people saw us, or at least him," he said, pointing at the scareman.

"Bah, I would hide better than you, you oversized mechanical monstrosity," the scareman sniped back.

Suddenly, there was a great flapping noise, and the three adventurers looked up at the black sky.

"There!" Achilles shouted, pointing into the swirling gray clouds.

Several flying creatures now came into view. They moved like bats and danced in the air, then began swooping low.

"Form a circle now!" Achilles ordered.

They stood back-to-back as the creatures began their descent. They had long leathery wings, shaggy bodies, and the faces of gorillas and howled and yelped as they swooped ever lower.

The creatures landed a few yards from the adventurers and slowly began to circle. They were larger than they first appeared, nearly six feet tall, barrel chested, with thick arms. Their eyes were red and long; jagged fangs jutted from their mouths. Their wings spread and flapped. Together, they formed a wall of gray and black flesh.

"Why are they looking at us like food?" Dorothy asked with a tremble in her voice as she raised her shotgun.

"They're blood feeders. They create the resurrected warriors for the witch. They serve the Necro Lord," the scareman answered. "The machine and I are no good to them, but you... Well, your human flesh is their favorite dish."

"Who is the Necro Lord? Why are you bringing him up now?"

"He is an ally to the witch. He once was a wizard, a real piece of human filth. These foul beasts are his servants, which is why most humans do not travel far from the cities," the scareman answered.

"Oh, great." Dorothy sighed as she took aim.

The creatures' wings stopped flapping, and they began to howl and cackle. One raised his hands, and the others stopped their celebration.

"The scareman lives?" it grunted. "The witch will be *very* happy to know this."

"I live, and you will die here and now!" the scareman shouted.

The creature laughed. "Our master has told us much of your weaknesses, your failures, your despair."

"Your master is a hack of magic and lies more than a thousand men," the scareman shot back.

"Our master can raise the dead and live forever, and you are made of straw and live off the remnants of prior days of glory," the creature hissed in return.

"Your master is a thief who sold his soul for any dark magic he could find in that mountain!" the scareman yelled. "He kills children for their life force to live... He is a monster, a coward and an ... asshole!"

Dorothy leaned over to Achilles. "Do you know anything about this little feud?"

"Not really. I know of the Necro Lord, but what I know is very little as I was built for war, not the squabbles of others."

"Gotcha," Dorothy said and focused back on the scareman.

"So, there is another wizard?"

"Bah, not a wizard, but a conman. A false prophet who used dark magic to lure both men and beasts under his control! Like these winged, simple-minded creatures!"

"Our master sent us to see if the rumors of a new machine and girl from another world were true. It looks like we found more than enough evidence for him and our queen," the creature grunted.

"You will bleed out quickly," Achilles chimed in.

"What strange hosts this girl keeps. Behold the mighty Achilles, free from his rusted bonds. No matter, the witch will have your head on her throne room wall in due time."

The scareman leaned into Dorothy. "The only way to kill them is to decapitate them, or stab wood through their heart."

"Okay, okay... vampires. We got those back home kinda, so we go for the head then."

"I may have a spell or two..." The scareman began to mumble and close his eyes.

"On my signal..." Achilles said.

The scareman's mind went blank for one second, but then several spells flooded his memory combined with images from Dorothy's books. Mathematics and science flooded his mind. And then dastardly distraction! For every spell that lent itself, a picture of a woman in a bikini holding a gun interrupted his chain of thought. He tried to refocus as the creatures began to flap their wings and howl once more.

The creatures moved closer, slowly screeching, taunting, as Conan barked with spit dripping from his jowls. He was ready to attack.

Without warning, one of the creatures screamed in horror as a large thick branch was thrust through his chest, spraying black fluids onto the blood-colored bricks below. It shook violently and fell over screaming, its wings flapping across the red brick pathway in desperation. One last howl and suddenly it turned to ash and collapsed into a pile of soot.

The creature to his left turned to see what happened and thus failed to see the blade coming from behind, and with a great thunking noise, the creature's head flew off and rolled at Dorothy's feet.

"Good Lord!" Dorothy yelled.

Something disappeared into the shadows as the remaining four creatures gathered together and began to hiss and scream.

"Something has them spooked," Achilles said.

"If it's frightening them... I definitely don't wanna see it," Dorothy said. "We may have to take off running!"

"Just wait," Achilles said. "Why didn't it attack us?"

Suddenly an arrow flew from the darkness and found the chest of another creature. It howled and fell to the ground. Its bloody hand pulled desperately on a thick arrow, and its body turned gray and collapsed into ashes.

"Whatever it is, it knows our enemy... We should help," Achilles said.

From all around, they could hear something running in the shadows, hiding between trees. The three remaining creatures started to run and flap their wings to take flight.

Something was hunting them.

"They will warn the witch!" the scareman yelled.

"No, they won't!" Dorothy said as she raised and fired the shotgun and then watched as one of the creatures fell to the earth with a screech.

"By the great maker!" Achilles yelled. "Nice shot, girl!"

The downed creature staggered to its feet and attempted to run unsteadily into the distance.

"They're getting away!" Dorothy said as she took off running, raising the shotgun as she chased the wounded creature down. It turned its head as she shot once more, tearing the creature's head from his body. Dorothy looked at the sky to spy the two remaining creatures well in flight. Dorothy sighed in despair.

From the darkness, however, a beast leaped from the woods and tackled the two creatures to the ground in a wild burst of fury. As the creatures howled, the beast struck them both again and again, their howls turning to whimpers and cries for mercy. A long blade was raised, and the beast lopped the heads from the creatures with a single strike.

The beast stood silent, its thick muscular back facing the adventurers. It was shaggy, with thick, gold-colored fur, and was menacing in the extreme. It then picked up the heads in one hand and raised its blade in the other. The beast slowly turned around and stared at the adventurers.

"Who is the monster in the Forest of The Damned? Who is the slayer of creatures... the protector of innocents? Whose name do they chant in the arena? Who is the king of the beasts?" he yelled.

He walked into view, his face that of a lion and his fangs glistening white as freshly fallen snow.

"I am Leo the Conqueror—Beast of the Woods and the greatest creature slayer of all time!"

"Oh, goodness!" Dorothy said as Leo approached. "He is magnificent!"

He walked with a swagger that revealed no fear. This self-proclaimed hero wore several pieces of armor and a chest plate atop his muscular physique. He dropped the creatures' heads to the ground with contempt and ran his pawlike hand through his long, flowing mane.

"No need for applause," he said. "Just doing what I do best, besides winning the hearts of the deafening crowds, and ladies." He winked at Dorothy. She blushed briefly.

"Oh, we definitely do not need this," the scareman said. "No, no, no."

"Is this who I think it is?" Achilles said, a bit wary in his tone.

"I am afraid so," the scareman said. "I thought he was dead or returned to what was left of his homeland."

"Well, who is he?" Dorothy asked. "He seems very interesting and very brave."

"I think it would be best if he told you who he is," Achilles noted, his red eyes flickering almost as if they rolled in frustration.

"Do you think he would let you?" the scareman said, smirking.

"Probably not..." Achilles replied.

Leo strutted some more as he approached.

"I, my dear, am Leo the Conqueror!" the lion announced as he took Dorothy's hand and gently kissed it. "And who might you be?" he asked her with a sweet smile.

"My name is Dorothy," she said, with just a hint of a blush on her cheeks.

"It is delightfully wonderful to meet such a beautiful female creature in such a dark and lonely environment. Pardon me a moment, my dear."

Suddenly Leo shifted his sights to the scareman as he stepped over to him and looked him up and down. He was head and shoulders taller than the scareman.

"So, I see you have changed," Leo stated. "Are you now made of straw? I heard the rumors but failed to believe until now. Last I saw of you, you were drunk as the witch carried you to her bedchambers within *my* castle on *my* island."

"A lot has changed, your Highness," the scareman mumbled.

"You know him?" Dorothy asked.

Before the scareman could open his mouth, Leo chose to explain. "I knew him as a man, not as a creature made of straw, and yet he has the same eyes ... the same dark eyes. And you, Achilles, General of the Iron Soldiers—your legend has grown."

"Well, I think not of myself as a legend..." Achilles began.

"Yes, I recall," said Leo. "You led the last attack of those willing to fight for justice ... and lost."

Achilles straightened up angrily, steam shot from his shoulders and back. "We were tricked by this traitor!" Achilles shouted as he grabbed the scareman by the shirt. "This coward is a liar! He made it rain! I was built for victory!"

"I never made it rain!" the scareman shouted and then mumbled a spell, and the iron hand suddenly released him. Achilles looked at his thick iron hands and growled. The scareman smirked; things were coming back.

The iron soldier let out a grunt, and steam sprayed from his neck bolts. "Whatever you say, liar."

The iron soldier then stood tall, walked up to Leo, and bent down to speak, like a mother addressing a child.

"Well, what I do remember that day was that you and your people were not there—the day of the great battle in the Forest of The Damned. Let's see, humans... dwarves... machines... a few fairies and one unicorn—I believe his name was Harold," Achilles said angrily. "Tell me, Scareman, from your view of the battlefield next to the witch, where you claim you did not make it rain as you watched us all slaughtered, did you spy any lions on that battlefield for the Eight Days of Darkness?"

The scareman looked up at the iron warrior, but then looked to Leo.

"I did *not* make it rain that day, and it was only five days of rain, not eight, or twelve, or twenty—these damned lies continue to follow me! Now that I think about it, I do not remember seeing any lions on that battlefield or in the forest during the war. Not even on the last day in the Forest of the Damned, where the witch was victorious and became ruler and queen of our world."

Leo cleared his throat. "I must have missed the invitation."

"In fact, I never saw any lions on any battlefield of any human city the witch conquered," the scareman added. "Almost as if they decided that a certain treaty and allies and loyalty did not matter because their land was so glorious and strong, and they knew that the witch would never double-cross them," he concluded with a smirk.

"Yikes," Dorothy whispered.

"How many months until the Land of the Lions fell?" Achilles asked.

"We fought very hard," Leo replied.

"And for how long?" the scareman asked, smirking.

"It took her eighteen months to overrun our islands... She used the resurrected warriors she created from dead humans and dwarves, wave after wave of them. I surrendered and suffered the indignity of being led away in chains in order to save those remaining. Now my land is nothing but tiny colonies hiding in caves."

"If you would have joined us, if you had kept your word, even in the rain we could have won," Achilles said. "You were a coward to the end, interested only in saving your own neck."

"I am the bravest in these lands!" Leo roared.

"Much better odds, indeed … had you shown up," the scareman said.

"Do you think it was easy after we fell? I was taken to her arena and fought for years, entertaining the lap dogs and sheep who now follow and help the witch! She killed my queen! I survived to fight and live another day. Even now, I do not know what she will do to the Land of the Lions since I escaped her clutches. She took everything from me! Me! The King of the Lions! Do you know who I am?"

"Get over yourself already," Dorothy said. "Who the hell does he think he is?"

Leo got in Dorothy's face and growled deeply. "I am Leo, King of the Land of the Lions and the Islands of the Mighty Mane."

"You do not have a crown on your head … or a land to rule. You are not my king. I don't care who you were or about tales of your glory. I am a free woman with my own damn problems. So, you can keep running and hiding in these woods, or you can come with us to retrieve the scareman's book and take revenge on the witch…"

"That is not part of the plan, Dorothy," the scareman said.

Leo snarled. He looked over at the scareman as he said, "I like her. I'm in."

"No, there is no *in*," the wizard said. "We do not need him. He won't fight."

Dorothy smiled. "Come on, he killed like five of those winged demons. I think we can definitely use him."

"He won't show up. He is a coward at heart," Achilles said.

Leo raged and grabbed the iron soldier by the chest plate, shoving the hulking machine back.

"I am not a coward, you rusting failure of metal and iron! I did what I thought was right!"

"You tried to save yourself!" Achilles shouted.

"And my people!" Leo shouted in return.

Achilles pointed to the scareman. "Even this liar did not try to save his own skin. He now is cursed because of his choice to rebel, and he is trying to make up for his errors. But you broke your word to save one of your nine lives... like a scared kitten."

Leo was about to leap at Achilles when the scareman placed his straw hand on Leo's broad shoulders.

Achilles snorted, and as steam shot from his thick bull neck, he walked over to a tree and sat down.

"I will go speak with him," the scareman said. "Though, in truth, I do not know if it is wise for you to come with us. Our journey may end in little more than death and hardship once more."

The scareman began to walk toward the resting iron general. Dorothy called to Conan, who was pissing on the decapitated head of a creature lying on the ground.

"I do not know if I am going to get home," she said with a shake of her head. "This is not how you get home."

The scareman stood in front of Achilles. "I have to get my book to fix the mistakes I made and to send her home. What do you want from me? How can I gain your trust?"

"You can't, not yet... but you can tell me and her all we need to know. Now look at us, with a coward of a lion among us. I almost prefer you over him." The iron soldier stood up, and steam drifted from his neck as he let out a sigh. "Start with honesty," he said, looking directly into the eyes of the scareman.

The scareman looked at Dorothy. "Dorothy, please come over here. We all need to talk. I need to tell you the truth."

"The truth?" Dorothy asked and quickly walked over to her companions. "If you can't send me home, then tell me now 'cause I'm tired and nearly done with all this! Vampires, lion people, resurrected warriors, dwarves, a witch, a straw wizard, a unicorn named Harold... I have nearly lost my mind in all of this..." she said as her eyes watered.

The scareman let out a sigh. "I *can* send you home... if I get my book back. But I need to tell you and Achilles the whole story—why it rained and where I have been. Until I confess all, I will never have your trust, and without trust, we will never win the day and get you home..."

"Okay," Dorothy said and sat down next to Achilles. "No lies!"

"No lies," the scareman said.

Leo stood off by himself, but when he noticed no one was paying any attention to him, he stepped over to the group.

"If you're going to speak of me, I would rather be present, so I can make sure it is the truth," he snarled.

"Can you account for what I'm going to tell them? So they will believe me?" the scareman asked.

"I don't know. I'll have to hear it all myself," Leo said.

"Then do join us, please," the scareman said.

"Okay, fine... but just remember, I'm not going to lie to them for you."

"Just join us, please... I need them to believe me, or our plans will be for naught."

Leo joined the group over by the tree. The scareman looked at Dorothy and Achilles and let out a sigh.

"Okay, this is the truth, I swear. No lies, no trickery, simply the story of the greatest wizard of all time—the story of the scareman."

Dorothy and Leo listened as Achilles just looked on ahead, almost ignoring his plea.

"Years ago, when I was young, I spent every spare hour studying magic. As I grew, I went to work for a great wizard named Claudian. He told me secrets of the land and of the sky. But as time passed, he failed in health, and, as I was his understudy, he gave me the chance of a lifetime. He offered me a book containing all his magic and knowledge. There was a catch however. I had to wait until the moon aligned with the sun."

"Oh, like an eclipse," Dorothy said.

"Yes, but I was young and overly eager, so when my teacher passed, I waited, and waited. I waited for weeks for the annual eclipse of the month of Henger. But something mysterious occurred, and the eclipse never came, as if something in the stars had been altered.

"I waited for the next eclipse, and that too never arrived, and again, and again, with no eclipse in sight. So, after ten years, I could wait no more... and I took the book on the night of a full moon and threw it open. Fire blazed forth, burning my face, arms, and hands. It disfigured me so badly I could no longer show my face and hands, so I began to wear a sackcloth and gloves and tried to fit into human society. Some thought I was ill or cursed, but as a wizard, we avoid most people anyway."

"What about the book?" Dorothy asked.

"Oh, it was fine, but my master had fooled me, and now I was cursed. As a disfigured freak, I could find no work with humans, but with my magic, I was really strong. A certain group of witches from the four winds took me in under their wings, and we began to work together. I had learned all I could, and with some of their help, I could read more of the book. I always hid the book from them. Can you imagine if women had the same power as men?"

Dorothy shot him a look.

"I mean..." the scareman said.

"Oh, the horror! That men and woman should be treated as equals!" she said with more than a hint of sarcasm.

"Sure, what good could come of this? But let me continue... when the humans made many machines to help with labor and travel, they relied less on people of magic, and we were rarely needed. Then they created the Iron Soldiers."

"We were needed to help humans," said Achilles.

"Well, either way, I was angry with the world of machines... I saw them as the downfall of our world, a mighty world of magic. They were building an army. Who were they going to fight? We had treaties with nearly everyone. Even the darkest magic users using the Black Mountain worked with good wizards. Things were running well for us people of magic for a short time. I was to be the one, the one who could bring all together. Instead, man used machines and then made machines for war. Many of the magic users in the world came together, some even stronger than myself, but I had the book, and so I still had control. I befriended the Witch of the North to save the world of magic and end the time of machines. Lies, propaganda, fear... All encroached on the witch's power, so even I was seduced. I mean, when I studied with her and her sisters, she always was kind to me. We bonded, and even though I was not handsome but burned horribly, she felt what I believed was affection toward me. Not many women would seduce a man in my condition. I know she is evil, but I was foolish."

"Okay, we get it. You were getting lucky a lot, and you were not used to it," Dorothy said.

"Humans are so strange when it comes to reproduction. It's easier to build a machine," Achilles said.

"Yeah, but that's not nearly as fun," the scareman countered.

"Too much information," Dorothy added.

"What?" the scareman said.

"Magic freak sex... gross. Please move on," Dorothy said.

Leo laughed.

"Fine, so it was not pure love exactly. Anyway, at the battle in the Forest of the Damned, I swear I had no knowledge of her intent to slaughter the dwarves and humans. She used me and fooled me, and many suffered for my foolishness."

"Ya ever think all that pillow talk was to find out about your magic powers, and you may have slipped up on the book?" Dorothy asked.

"I told her about the book, eventually."

"Ah yes, honey potted. A burned wizard with the social skills of a cactus has some hot witch digging him when suddenly his magic is just the best ever, and after a while, she gets what she wanted. Dude... really?" Dorothy said.

"Can I finish?" the scareman asked.

"Go ahead.... I hate this witch even more now," Dorothy said. "She is a gold-digging piece of shit."

"When the war was won, nearly all users of magic were captured, killed, or tossed aside, so she alone could rule."

"And she put me in chains," Achilles reminded.

"Yes, after that, I returned to the witch's castle for several months before deciding I was done with her and her dark servants. She had enslaved most of the world and killed off nearly all users of magic, and I knew it was only a matter of time before I was to be made an example of. She also spent more and more time with the Necro Lord, that hack! But she had other plans... She sensed my betrayal, and when I was sneaking out to escape with the book, I was captured." The scareman's voice took on an air of pure rage. "She had told me she would return me to my human form, but never did. As a punishment for my attempted escape, she weaved a spell of clouded mind from my book and ordered her flying blood-feeding creatures to fly me out of the castle, where they ripped me to shreds and dropped me, scattering my limbs to the ground."

"How awful!" Dorothy said.

"Well… I survived to heal my straw body using a few spells I could remember and have lived in hiding from her and all humans and dwarves ever since. I have a few spells memorized, but I am so out of practice. Her spell to fog my mind has fortunately been fading ever since, but it is still very difficult to focus."

"So, you never sent for me, or anyone… You lied about that, too?" Dorothy said.

"Yes and no. I did not know what the winds I created would bring me. All I knew was that you were not from this world, and I hoped you could assist me in my quest to retrieve my book. You have surprised me, Dorothy. I sent out that spell to bring a champion from another land, and you have proven you are certainly such a champion. I now truly believe we can succeed in our quest."

Leo let out a large yawn. "Well, that's all nice and dandy, but what about me?"

"What about you?" the scareman asked.

"Well, doesn't she need to know about me? I mean… she has to have heard of me—Leo the Conqueror!"

"She is not from our world, Leo," Achilles said. "And I know enough already. I can tell her more if need be."

The scareman looked at the iron general. "You are so stubborn; you think because you're such a great leader, that as you were built, you know all the answers… Well, you don't. I never made it rain and…"

"Ssshhh…" Leo said as he turned his ears and sniffed the air. "Something is coming. I can smell a strong scent. Be on guard. I think…" He sniffed again. "Yes, it's the creatures of the witch. I could smell their foul odor a hundred yards away."

"How many?" the scareman asked.

"I'm not sure... enough to cause concern. Maybe they have been tracking you. Maybe they heard of our little battle."

"Okay, let's get moving. The remains of the Diamond City are just a couple of miles north," Achilles said.

Dorothy looked into the night sky and saw four small dots approaching. "No, they're gonna be here soon... look!" she said as she pointed to the sky.

"Time to march out!" Achilles said, as he stood with a creak.

A beeping sound, followed by a metallic voice, caught them all by surprise. "Kill the witch and save the world!"

Dorothy grunted and pulled out her cell phone. "I really need to delete this game."

"Maybe it wants you to kill the witch?" Achilles asked. "We machines are very clever."

"Not this one. It's just wanting me to spend money to play it, so it runs ads about things I cannot afford to buy," Dorothy said and slid her phone away. "Do you want to come with us to the Diamond city?" Dorothy asked Leo.

"Hmmmm..." he growled. "It has certainly been a while. So many humans fear me... and respect me, also, of course. If the word got out, I was alive, she may hunt me again."

"Aw, come on, it's not like you're gonna make any friends with these two," she said, rolling her eyes at the scareman and Achilles.

"You have a point, and an adventure may be good for my blood. Besides, I could use a warm meal and a drink. It has been a very different life for me in these woods."

"Well, one thing I know is it's going to be very hard to hide as we move about the city," Achilles said. "We should stay on the outside, perhaps."

"Good, then it's settled. We're off to the Diamond City. We will try to get the book after we rest, and you guys can get along," Dorothy said with a smile as she walked back on the brick road with Conan loyally beside her.

The scareman let out a sigh, and a large iron hand landed on his shoulder. "At least she has some fight in her and is as stubborn as we are," Achilles noted in encouragement.

"True, but that's just what I'm afraid of," the scareman said, smiling.

# CHAPTER 11

## "THE MIGHTY LAIR"

The Necro Lord stood at the entrance of his lair staring at the twin moons. Years ago, he would have enjoyed such a night, so calm, so peaceful, but now clouds rolled quickly across the sky, and rain could be seen falling in the distance. He remembered clear nights, and he remembered the sun, too. He remembered the choices he had made, and his newfound power outweighed the despair growing in his heart. Power was more satisfying to him than any sunrise.

Three winged creatures appeared in view, breaking his train of thought. It was not the patrol he had sent, however, and they carried a leather sack.

The creatures landed and laid the sack at his feet. "It was a difficult hunt, Master. The humans are wise to our ways and are hiding their children. They seem to be growing more and more cunning," the creature grunted.

The Necro Lord bent down and opened the sack to spy a young girl, rubbing her eyes.

"Mommy?" she said. "I'm so tired!"

"She took the candy and fell asleep. She gave us little trouble," the creature added.

"Well, let's make this quick then," the Necro Lord said. He took the child's hand. The little girl looked up, but instead of the Necro Lord, she saw a woman in a white robe.

"Are you taking me to my bed?" she asked sweetly.

"Yes. Now come with me, so you can get some much needed sleep," the woman in white replied.

The Necro Lord and his creatures walked back into his lair with the little girl holding the Necro Lord's hand. He led the girl deep into the lair, to a back room with a large wooden table. Bookshelves lined the walls and potions sat in dull glass bottles.

"Here is your bed, sweetheart," the woman in white said, and the little girl crawled on the table.

"So tired... I just want Mommy and sleep," she said. "Can I have more of that candy in the morning? It was yummy."

"Yes," said the woman in white. "Now close your eyes and sleep."

The little girl obeyed and was soon snoring.

"That magic candy is so much easier than the crying, screaming, and fighting," the Necro Lord said.

"I remember. The old ways were far more difficult," the creature said.

"Well, at least we do not need to do this as often now that the witch has won. We do not need their essence to raise the dead. It's much better this way. We only need a child every few weeks to maintain the witch's hold on her resurrected army."

"Your army is full of poopy faces and booger men!" shouted a voice.

The Necro Lord looked up as the ghosts of several children stood in the cave entrance.

"Ah, good. You are here. For once, I want you to see what I do to troublemaking children and why you should stop bothering me!" the Necro Lord said.

"We know what you do, poopy head!" the lead boy said.

"Well, good. I am going to give you a new friend, and you can tell her everything." The Necro Lord then lifted his hands and began to chant. Swirls of green and blue began to fall like soft feathers from the ceiling and covered the little girl. She began to sparkle, and silver shards of dust rose from her frail body. She did not scream, but twitched like she was dreaming. The shards floated above her form and slowly moved over her body to a glass tube covered in symbols and diamond shards. The Necro Lord continued until the blue and green mist covered the girl, and the dust stopped rising from her body.

Suddenly the girl was still, and the mist faded away. A lone tear rolled down her pale cheek. The Necro Lord then collapsed to the table and groaned. The creatures raced to him and helped him to his feet.

"Master?" the lead creature grunted.

"I will be fine. It is done." He looked over to the children, and the little girl now stood next to the boy.

"He is an evil man," the little girl said. "He lied to me. I want to go home. Where is the lady in the white dress? I want my mommy!"

The little boy took her hand. "He is a very evil man. But for now, you have to stay with us. We get to play all day, and you will never feel pain again."

The Necro Lord smiled and stood up. "That's right, and I will live forever." He then stumbled from the room with the demons behind him. "Stupid children," he muttered. "The only downside to this magic mountain is those blasted child ghosts and constant harassment!"

The little boy looked at the young girl, who stared at her body on the wooden table.

"He only thinks he will live forever," the boy said to comfort her. "We have seen the future... He will come and play with us soon. There is a game we need to teach you; it's very fun. We call it 'Rip and Tear,' and someday soon that poopy head is going to come play it with us."

"How do you know? He seems so strong?" the little girl asked.

"This place is really fun; it is magic, and it tells us secrets—and tells us not to tell the adults."

"Really?" she replied.

"Yes. Now come with us. I want you to meet some more new friends. So many secrets, it's so fun to play here! He thinks he is so powerful, but he does not understand the magic of the mountain like we do."

The ghosts of the children disappeared deep into the caves, and the little girl listened to the voices of the mountain as they whispered. She then laughed as she followed them.

"He *is* a big poopy face," she said with a smile.

"We will have such fun with him..." the boy ghost said.

# "I HAVE THE MUNCHIES"

**D**orothy and her newfound allies walked on through the darkened Forest of the Damned and, after an hour, found themselves on a large hill. Looking down, they saw the remains of a city. Several tower structures that looked like stone pillars rose to the sky with a wooden wall surrounding the buildings. Small lights could be seen flickering, lighting up the town's massive stone buildings.

"Wow, it's beautiful," Dorothy said.

"That place is a hole in the ground," Leo snorted. "My capital city on our largest island was three times as big, with riches, jewel-covered buildings, and towers to the heavens. Our island paradise was unlike anyone had seen... until she invaded."

"You had jewels covering the buildings? Wow, that's a lot of money in any world," Dorothy said.

"Yes, the dwarves mined them and helped build the Diamond City and the Ruby City as well... but the witch destroyed the Ruby City, and then we had the three days of darkness, or five ... or seven. Everyone has a different truth over time."

"Why hasn't she destroyed the Diamond City?" Dorothy asked.

"She likes to keep a strong grip on the people. She gives them a life of slavery—or death!" Achilles answered.

"We in our world would fight for freedom," Dorothy said angrily. "Death is just a part of fighting for the freedoms of others."

"Yes, but here if you die, the witch uses her power, and you become one of the resurrected warriors. Others she just uses as food for her army. It's very sad; you live and live again. Only the dead who cannot be raised feel peace," the scareman noted.

"That's really awful," Dorothy said.

"Yes, so the humans just exist in this city from day to day. They have food and shelter, but in truth, they are little more than slaves and must do whatever the witch commands," Leo added. "She offers them an illusion of freedom. She provides food and entertainment via gladiatorial fights and other entertainment. She keeps them on a leash, and they do not resist."

"Bread and circuses..." started Dorothy.

"What?" asked Leo.

"Oh... it's nothing, just something I learned in school."

They walked down the hill as some traces of the red bricks remained. They began to cut through a thick large field that seemed to grow wildly across the hillside. The plants had heavy green leaves and thin stems. Conan frolicked ahead and sniffed around eagerly.

"So, what could happen in this city? I mean, if the humans hate you all, we may get thrown out, right?" Dorothy asked.

"They will not throw us out. Kill us maybe... but I have a friend in town—if he is still alive. It's been over a decade," Achilles said. "I do not know if he lives. He was on that battlefield my last day... but he had a tavern years ago. So, we will go there."

"What about the guards?" Dorothy asked.

"Leave them to me," the scareman said. "I think I have a spell of sleep. I will try to get us in. If not, I know of a spell of confusion. If it is successful, they will think we are someone else. But once inside, well, we better stick to back alleyways and shadows."

Dorothy looked around and sniffed the air. "What is that smell? It's so familiar, like home... It's weak, but I swear I know it."

"Oh." Leo smiled. He pulled up a small green leafy plant. "See these? They call this the hungry plant. People burn them in their homes; it gives off a strange aroma, makes humans feel very relaxed, and forget their troubles."

"Really? Is that why there is a field of it just outside the city?" Dorothy asked.

"Yes, some people can be much more docile when they are feeling... well, a little fuzzy," Leo added.

Dorothy pulled one of the plants from the ground and held it up to her nose. "You burn this?"

"Well, the humans do. It does nothing for me," Leo replied.

"Oh my God!" Dorothy said. "I know this stuff... it's weed!"

"No, it's a plant of many uses, it is no weed..." began the scareman.

"No." Dorothy smiled. "Back home, it's called marijuana."

"Marijuana?" the scareman said. "What a silly name for a plant."

Dorothy laughed. "Yeah, it makes you relaxed and hungry. It makes food taste awesome. I've only smoked it a couple of times, but we definitely have it back home.

One of my customers at work actually sells it. Humans put it in all kinds of things, oils and even food. Most humans I know smoke it, though."

"You smoke it?" Leo asked. "In a pipe?"

"Well, yeah, kinda. This stuff is illegal in many places in my world. Some places, however, use it for medicine." Dorothy looked at the massive field and shook her head.

"Wow, talk about getting high—this place could satisfy all of California."

"I cannot believe a plant would be outlawed. It must be because of machines," the scareman said. "Nature is for us all to enjoy."

"Well, yeah... sometimes humans forget what nature is. We have a lot of machines, and we destroy our plants and world slowly. Not all humans in my world do the right thing. Some of them are as greedy as the witch."

"So, the machines are destroying your world as well," the scareman said.

"No, we humans are doing that on our own," Dorothy said and smiled at Achilles. "Machines are just fine. Now, let's get out of this field before I get the munchies." Dorothy dropped the plant and tightened the backpack over her shoulder. "Hmm... the hard part will be getting through the gates with Achilles. If machines are banned, they will spot him."

"I could send you to the tavern. Just let them know I am free and on the outside of the city walls," Achilles suggested.

"If there is trouble in a tavern at night, I will definitely need you around," Dorothy said. "Not stuck outside, unable to get to us."

Leo crossed his arms and looked over his shoulder. "You do not think I could aid in a bar fight?"

"That's not the point. It's his contacts we need him there for. If we get into the city, he can hide in the alleyways. He needs to be with us. Hey, Stitch-face, what about a spell to hide, something like invisibility?"

The scareman pondered a moment. "Maybe... wait... no."

"What?"

"His metal cannot be cloaked. He is thousands of pounds of iron and steel! I was once that powerfully good, but now, I do not think so."

"Well, we need to hide him, or make a disguise," Dorothy said.

"How do you hide a machine this large?" Leo asked.

Dorothy began to wander in a circle. "If we conceal him... or make him into something else... I have an idea!" she said with a grin.

The gate to the decaying city was enormous, built of tree trunks and thick ropes. All along the walls were wooden and iron spikes. Two guards, one on each side of the great gate, watched from platforms inside the city walls. Torches lit their posts as they looked out into the darkness.

Dorothy rode on Achilles's back as branches and leaves were tied to his shoulders and legs. The scareman and Leo pushed on his thighs from behind as the great iron warrior crawled reluctantly.

"This is most embarrassing. I never saw myself ever pretending to be a wagon," Achilles grunted.

"A *broken* wagon that we have to push," the scareman added.

"Quiet, it will work," Dorothy said. "Just be cool."

"Oh, I can be cool," Achilles said, still not understanding how his temperature would aid them.

Dorothy and her companions slowly approached and waited in front of the gate.

"Better get that spell going, oh great wizard," Leo mumbled.

"I'm getting to it... hold on," the Strawman said and continued to meditate.

Dorothy called to the guards, "Hello, excuse me, could you allow us in?"

Neither of the guards moved.

Dorothy was tired, and her patience was almost gone. "Hey! Down here! Can you let us in, please?"

The two guards just looked ahead, and one rubbed his nose.

"I think they're ignoring us," Leo said. "That's the worst. Besides, it is so late there is no way they're gonna let travelers in. We may have to camp outside the city 'til dawn."

"Hey?" Dorothy screamed.

One of the guards looked down.

"Yeah, that's right, bozo, we're down here... Can you let us in?"

"Sorry miss... No entrance after dark, city law, imposed by the witch herself. Come back in the morning."

"Please sir, our wagon is broken, and our horse lies dead in the forest. We desperately need shelter."

The two guards looked at one another as if they may just break.

The scareman began a chant and then smiled. "Ask again Dorothy."

"Okay. Hello, can you please let us into the city?"

One of the guards looked at Dorothy and her travelers... He then started laughing and didn't stop.

"Hey, this isn't funny. We need to get inside!" she said angrily.

"Oh, really? With that broken wagon. Look at that wagon... It's so funny!" said the other guard, who began to laugh as well. The two began to laugh so hard they both were leaning on the wall, and then they began to mock Dorothy.

"You want in this city?" The guards howled with laughter.

"What kind of spell was that?" Dorothy asked.

"Well, not the one I thought apparently," the scareman said.

The two men laughed louder and began to make faces at the travelers.

"Oh, look at me, I am poor a wee girl with a broken wagon and ugly friends..." the guard said as he fell over laughing.

"Well, get rid of that spell... It's like they're drunk."

"Okay, sorry about that... I'll try something else."

The scareman began to chant again, and without warning, the two guards fell over and disappeared.

"Sweet dreams, boys," the scareman said.

"That's great... now how are we gonna open the gate?" Leo asked.

"Well, I thought the machine could lift it... it lifted Dorothy's truck," the scareman said.

"What?" Achilles asked. "You want me to break into the city?"

"You're an outlaw to the witch, and you're worried about breaking into the city? Can you lift the gate or not?" the scareman asked.

"I can... but not enough to get in."

"What if one of us crawls under... if the three of you lift it just a foot or two, I could slide under and open it," Dorothy suggested.

"No, that would not work. Leo may be able to turn the wheel to raise it, but it takes two full-grown men to raise the chains," Achilles said.

"We don't have much time. I'm sure someone will notice that the guards are gone soon. If we are going to do something, do it," Leo barked. "I'll raise the gates."

"Hey Stitch-face, can't you change the matter or something, like you did with my bow?" Dorothy asked. "Could you make the gate lighter?"

"Well, yes, I could, or at least I will try," the scareman said with a smile.

Achilles and Leo ran to the gate and grabbed near the bottom as Dorothy got down on her hands and knees. The scareman in the back began to whisper enchanting words once more.

"Hope he does not make the gate drunk, or heavier..." Leo said.

"Okay, on three," Dorothy said.

"Three!" said Achilles and began to lift. Leo was surprised but began to lift, as well. The gate slowly inched its way up. The two warriors began to grunt under the strain as the scareman finished his spell. The gate was raised just enough for Leo to roll under, and he did so with feline speed.

Achilles then dropped the gate with a soft thud. The scareman walked over and staggered, dropping to one knee.

"That spell took a lot out of me. I'm sorry I couldn't do more. Some spells are stronger than others."

"It's a mighty gate. I'm just glad you didn't make us laugh or put us to sleep," Achilles said.

Once inside, Leo located the chained handle and began to turn the massive wheel that pulled the gate into the air. He grunted and struggled a bit as the gate rose a few inches at every turn. When the gate was high enough, Dorothy and the scareman crawled underneath.

The three began to lift the gate higher to let Achilles inside the city as well. The iron general laid flat and squirmed under the massive gate and finally got his whole body through. Once he was inside, the three lowered the gate slowly back down.

"See that? We worked together and…" Dorothy began.

"And we're exhausted," Leo said as he bent over and took a breath or two.

"Hey, at least we made it inside," Dorothy said.

Achilles joined the others by the massive wheel. "No time for rest. Let's get to the tavern. We can rest there if my friends still live."

The other three slowly stood up, stretched, and followed the iron general as he did his best to hide in the shadows and make little noise. They slowly made their way from alleyway to alleyway in the darkness of candle-lit streets, and they disappeared deeper into the Diamond City.

Within her stone castle, the witch peered out a small arched window to spy on all of her barren domain. The night had produced several stars that could only be seen as the clouds shifted. Her lust for power had given her everything she desired, but a small part of her wished to see the sun more often. It was magic keeping the rain here, and when it did not rain, the sun would come out for only a few minutes a week. This affected the plants, the food, and the humans. They were harder to placate than she had believed they would be. Her balance of fear, plus the free time they had with the hungry plants, kept most in control. Magic was once again growing in most areas, and she would continue to be in charge.

"Are you looking for something?" said a weak voice. "Something you still cannot have, even with all your power?"

The witch spun around toward a woman chained to a thick wooden table. Her eyes were cold, but she still hung on to life. Her frail body had scars and dried blood on her bare legs and arms. Her white dress was shredded with deep red stains of dried blood.

The witch smiled. "Oh, my sister. I thought you had joined the others?" the witch said as she looked at two more tables. One held a skeleton and the other a corpse, with several flies circling. Both bodies were still bound in chains.

"Soon, my sister, soon. When you join us," she said weakly. "As loving as we were to you, you still betrayed us, your own flesh and blood. We were a team, we were a family, and you and that wizard decided that magic was better than family."

"Bah, family? The three of you always kept me in the dark, always planning, hiding… I am the Witch of the North, and you three Witches of the West, South, and East never gave me the respect I deserved. You always treated me as an inferior. Well, not now. No, now I am the last of the Regions of Witches, and I am queen of this land." She walked down three stone steps deeper into the dungeon, approached the Witch of the West, and caressed her sunken cheek. "It will not be long before death comes to carry you away, sweet Sister."

"Nor for you. I had a vision…"

"You do not see the future anymore, only fantasies."

"I saw a machine fall from the sky, a mighty machine, and a girl controlling it. She will bring redemption and honor back to the land of humans and bring true balance between magic and machine."

The witch laughed and then swiftly smacked the Witch of the West across the face.

"No one will take my power, no one! Your visions are nothing! If you could see the future, then why did you not foresee your fate? Or the fate of our sisters? Or stop me?"

"I was hoping you would stop yourself. I believed in the good in you, Sister," the Witch of the West answered.

The queen stepped from the table. "There was no machine that fell from the sky controlled by some girl. Magic is here, and this world is mine."

One of the walls of stone began to shift in color, and suddenly a faded glass oval appeared.

The witch walked to the wall. "What is it?" she asked angrily.

In the cloudy glass, the Necro Lord stood tall. "My Queen, they did not find what you were seeking, but my other spies found the remains of my creatures. Something, or someone, killed them. It may be the girl in that machine."

"Ha!" the Witch of the West shouted. "Perhaps you are not as powerful as you believe, my sister."

"Shut up!" the queen shouted. "Send more spies—I want the girl alive, find her, and destroy the machine. As for the girl, bring her to me."

"Yes, my Queen," the Necro Lord replied.

In the background, three children pointed at the mirror. "He has a poop-faced girlfriend!" one shouted.

"A poop-faced girlfriend with a pumpkin head!" shouted another little girl.

"Sod off, you vile children!" the Necro Lord screamed, and the ghosts of the children ran off into the caves.

The witch moved her hand over the wall, and the mirror disappeared. "I hate his lair and those horrible little children."

"So my visions are just my imagination and fantasies, then?" the Witch of the West asked.

"If you tell me more, I may spare you... Tell me what you can, and maybe the resurrected dead will not eat your flesh like they did our sisters," the queen said.

"My visions only show so much, and being in such a weak state, I just... I just cannot see more. Maybe some food, some medicine... and my strength may return," she said with a weak grin.

The queen walked over and spat in her face. "No. You will die here, and you will never see me lose power!" The witch stormed out of the dungeon, slamming the thick door behind her.

The Witch of the West closed her eyes and whistled. A small bird flew into the window and placed a crust of bread in her mouth. "So, what else have you seen, little one?" she asked as she chewed.

The bird chirped and danced on the Witch of the West's frail body.

"Really... he is free? Well, this just keeps getting better. Bring me some hungry plant to chew on. The pain grows each day, and I must stay alive to see her die."

The small bird then fluttered out the window, and the Witch of the West smiled her first smile in a long time.

# CHAPTER 14

## "TROUBLE IN THE TAVERN"

The small band of travelers made their way through the darkened backstreets of the Diamond City. Achilles's gears and cylinders creaked as he tried to move with stealth, but without result.

"He is so loud!" the scareman said.

"It is only because we are trying to be quiet," Dorothy shot back.

Dorothy looked behind her as they continued into the shadows. "I hope your friend is still alive," she said in a whisper to Achilles. "Even if he is, will we be safe? Look at who is with us?"

"If he is alive, we will be safe. He was friends with the blacksmith who forged me and the others. Besides, humans that hang about in taverns this late are normally a wanted breed... unless a spy for the witch is there, we should be safe," Achilles said.

They walked on and crossed two more alleyways until Achilles stopped and pointed across the dirt and brick street to a line of buildings. "There it is, The Lucky Stone Tavern, the third building on the left."

"Well, great, now what? Do we just stroll in... or make a reservation, perhaps?" Leo grunted.

"No. Dorothy will enter and try to find him... The rest of us will sneak around back and wait."

"How am I gonna find him? I don't know who he is, or what he looks like!"

"Just go in and ask around. His name is Killian. He is a tall, lanky fellow. Um... no scars... hmmm, this could be tougher than I thought."

"Yeah, I gotta find a guy who I've never seen and whose face you can't quite describe," Dorothy said.

"Just go to the bar," Achilles said. "Ask around. If he is still alive, people will know of him. If not, we must leave the city quickly."

"Okay, fine," Dorothy said as she handed Leo her shotgun. "I'm taking my pistol with me, but I'll leave this with you. The last thing I need is to stand out."

"We will be right here waiting. If you need help, we will be ready," said Leo. "You better be ready. A girl not from around here, walking into a tavern late at night. It's not safe."

"Don't worry," Achilles said. "Just go to the bar and ask for Killian."

Dorothy tightened her backpack to her shoulders. She glanced at the front of the tavern.

A sign hung from a wooden pole outside the door, reading "Ale and Good Times!" Below the lettering lay a hungry plant with a huge smiley face drawn on.

"Well, here goes," Dorothy said. She walked to the door, slowly opened it, and entered with a wish and a prayer.

The tavern was dimly lit with candles and was decorated with crude paintings along the walls. There were tables sporadically arranged and people clustered together, drinking and laughing. Several women in small fur-covered outfits scurried around with pitchers. There was a hint of the hungry plant in the air, Dorothy noted as she looked around the tavern, trying to locate the bar. She had been in worse places. Not a dive, but not exactly where you'd take your parents for a quiet drink. This was a local fun tavern, not as rough as she'd imagined, but still, she walked tall and kept her head on a swivel for good measure.

Suddenly the bar grew quiet, and Dorothy looked around to find she was discovered by the tavern visitors. Nervous from the eyes of dozens of patrons, she blurted out. "I need an ale... Any man here man enough to buy a woman a drink?"

Many of the men roared with laughter as others went back to their drinking. Dorothy was relieved. Most were just here to drink themselves into a drunken stupor and did not seem bothered by the appearance of a stranger. She walked deeper into the large room and looked for the bar, which she found near the back of the tavern. After walking briskly over and dodging waitresses, she arrived. The bartender, a short stocky man wearing a green shirt and white apron, smiled at Dorothy. "Well, well, what would you like, young lady?"

"Nothing yet... Actually, I'm looking for someone."

"Well, I could be someone."

*Good Lord,* Dorothy thought. *Even in other worlds, men are still men.* Dorothy smiled a sweet smile as she leaned in. "Oh, I bet you say that to all the women who come in here."

"No, just the pretty ones," he retorted.

"Well, maybe you can help me. I need to find Killian."

"Oh, of course. My boss has all the pretty women looking for him. Hold on, I'll be right back."

The man turned and disappeared into the back room. Dorothy was relieved it appeared to be that simple to find Achilles's friend and let out a sigh and then a yawn.

She slowly pulled her cell phone from her pocket and glanced at it. Nearly midnight, it was at 64% power. She slid her phone away. She was exhausted, spied, and then sat on a bar stool.

"If the lady is wanting a drink... I can get her one," a boastful voice said.

Dorothy turned and found a grimy-looking man, with animal skins for a shirt and a gruff face as he smiled, revealing his half tooth-filled smile.

"Let me buy you a drink, little woman... and maybe I'll buy you a night in an inn as well."

Realizing this man was just a pitiful drunk, Dorothy gave a polite "No, thank you, maybe another time."

Angered, the man grabbed Dorothy by the arm tightly and shouted, "No! Do you know who I am? I fought in the battle of three armies and in the Forest of the Damned. The girl says no to me, after all me and my men tried to do for this world? You *will* let me buy you a drink!" the man demanded.

From the back room, the young man returned and behind him followed a lanky man with blue eyes and a limp.

"Let the girl go, Dunn. Can't you see she is not from this city, maybe from the Emerald City, I'm guessing, I mean... look at her strange clothing," the man with the limp suggested.

Angered even more, the drunk yelled his reply, "Oh, far be it from me to be hospitable to a woman, or per-haps she is a new slut for you, Killian?"

"That's enough, Dunn. Now have another on the house. The war is over. Our war ended years ago."

Dunn looked around and smiled his half-toothed smile. "On the house," he mumbled, and then looked around.

"You're Killian?" Dorothy asked.

"Yes, and seeing I have no idea who you are, I assume someone sent you here. Look, my days of bootlegging ale and weapons are well over. I have my tavern and my friends. The witch checks in often, and we do not need any more trouble round here. If you're here for any of that, I must ask you to leave, or I will sic Dunn on you."

"I was told by a friend to ask for you, a friend who thinks very highly of you," Dorothy said.

"You know, Killian..." Dunn interrupted. "I think you underestimate me sometimes."

Killian looked over at Dunn. "Listen, I don't want trouble. Just go and have an ale on me, okay?"

"No, I think I'll have a drink, and I also think I will take the girl with me."

Dorothy looked at Dunn. "I'm sorry, sir. I'm just not interested. Please leave me alone. I have walked far and am very tired."

Dunn then grabbed Dorothy's arm a second time and yelled, "You are coming with me!"

The bar grew quiet.

Killian took out a dagger and swiftly pointed it at Dunn's neck. "Don't make me do this, Dunn... you know I will if I have to."

Dunn grinned and then began laughing. "Hear that, boys? He wants to fight me. Finally, the wounded captain of the Diamond Militia has the stones to fight once more."

Close to a dozen men in the tavern rose from their tables and slowly made their way to Dunn. Many had swords hanging from their belts.

"I hope those are your bouncers," Dorothy mumbled to Killian.

"What's a bouncer?"

"Oh great, an old-fashioned testosterone-fueled bar fight. Great, this is just what I need."

Killian backed off with the dagger and looked at his bartender, who held a small axe in his hand and seemed ready to go down swinging.

"Well, now, little lady. Are you going to let me buy you a drink… and maybe more… or do I have to wreck this tavern and kill a lot of innocent people?" Dorothy let out a sigh and smiled at Dunn.

"Achilles!" she screamed.

"Achilles?" Killian mumbled in astonishment, and just then a giant thud echoed in the bar. The front door rocked from its hinges and was tossed to the floor in the middle of the bar as the iron general stormed in, ripping the stone walls, sending rubble to the floor. Achilles stepped into the bar as dust rose and steam shot from his neck, Leo to his left with his sword drawn and the scareman to his right holding the shotgun. The three stood battle ready, looking around for Dorothy.

Killian looked at the three intruders as the bar fell silent and all eyes fixed on them.

"Dorothy!" Leo shouted.

The young woman pushed Dunn away and raised her hand above Dunn's mob. "I'm over here… and I found Killian."

The three warriors walked with their heads high and chests out and seemed to give dirty looks to the tavern's patrons. Conan walked along slobbering and seemed to smile, ready for a good fight. Dunn's men moved out of the way eagerly as the iron general walked through the crowd, while Leo growled and sneered.

"Achilles? How? By what magic are you alive?" Killian asked.

"This young girl saved me from the Forest of the Damned. I owe her my life. I was still as a statue, but my magic spark was never extinguished."

Killian then pointed to the scareman. "What is he doing here?" The scareman tightened the grip on the shotgun, though he still had no idea how to use it.

"He claims to be able to send this young woman home... She is lost and from a faraway land. We hoped to come here for a night of rest," Achilles said.

Killian looked at the patrons as they began to leave quickly.

"You have grand timing, my old friend, but time is short. Some of these in here may tell of your freedom, but I have room for you for one night. You must make haste by dawn. The witch has eyes everywhere. You may all stay but... as for the scareman..."

"What?" the scareman asked

"No, he is with us, with me," Dorothy said. "He has to stay with us."

"She is right... though I do not know whether he is trustworthy," Achilles added.

The scareman threw up his hands. "I have just about had it with all of this hatred toward me. I am sorry for what I did, but I have paid quite a price for my selfishness—I have very little memory of my magic, my body is straw, and I have been hiding from the witch for several years with no help from anyone. I am so tired of the blame... I am trying to fix my mistakes and..."

Leo put his pawlike hand on his shoulder. "Calm yourself, Scareman. If they will not have you, then I will go with you."

"No. We all are staying or leaving, that's it. I will sleep in the street... I don't care. We are together," Dorothy said.

Killian looked at Achilles. "Are we safe? I am well aware of his powers."

"He is safe. Just an old, feeble man. Trust me on that," Achilles laughed.

"Old and feeble?" the scareman said. "Who lifted the gate... and who helped Dorothy save you from those trees?"

"Okay," Achilles said with a grin. "Just old. He still has some tricks. I will rest with one eye open."

Leo let out a chuckle, and the scareman turned and gave a frown. "If I had my book and was flesh and bone again, I would show you all."

"Lighten up, Scareman. We're all tired. Let's just call it a night," Leo said.

"You are all welcome to stay. I have a few rooms upstairs you can sleep in. If I hear of trouble, however, you must all be ready to leave in haste. There are spies everywhere," Killian said.

Suddenly another group of men stormed into the tavern. "Dunn!" a man shouted. "We heard there was trouble."

Dunn was now seated in the corner and looked around as thirty men awaited his orders.

He got up and walked over to Achilles.

"Well, if you cannot lead on a field of battle, then I don't see how you can lead in a tavern. I never liked your plan or your kind. Bringing your iron skull to the witch will gain me much favor. I could own this tavern in a few days..."

"What is this? Some kinda gang turf thing?" Dorothy asked.

The men encircled the small group with their backs to the bar. The three warriors pulled their weapons and looked ready for a fight.

"I want the girl!" Dunn shouted. "Maybe the witch would pay me well... even after I have my way with her."

"No one is having their way with me. That I can tell you now, you cretin," Dorothy said angrily as she pulled her pistol.

Killian pulled a sword from behind the bar and looked at the men angrily.

"You have no chance!" Dunn said, "We outnumber you six to one."

"Good Lord! I do not need any more of this macho bullshit!" Dorothy said angrily.

"We are not normal men. We are warriors and have fought harder and stronger than the likes of you," Leo snorted.

"You did not show up on the battle of the Forest of the Damned or any fight for our world. Hiding in your island retreat, I heard, so you are still just a coward," Dunn said.

Leo let out a growl, which caused the men to back down for a split second.

"Oh, we may not kill the iron warrior, but we can kill the girl and your friend behind the bar. As for the scareman, we will burn him easily enough, and the lion is strong, but not against a dozen fighting men."

"Older, out-of-practice, drunken fighting thugs," Leo said, smirking. "You mock my past and instead dwell in past glories."

The scareman handed Dorothy the shotgun. He raised his hands and began to mumble, the words dark and crude in nature.

The tension in the bar was overwhelming as the warriors began to square off.

"If this is what you truly want, then we will fight you," Achilles said. "You will bleed first, that I can promise."

"And you and your friends will die," Dunn said angrily.

"I would not be too sure of that," said a loud, gruff voice.

The whole bar turned to the shattered doorway as Brawner and a dozen dwarves, all wielding axes and war hammers, walked in quickly.

The humans were now in the middle of a fight they knew they would lose. The dwarves just smiled and raised their weapons, chanting, "The thrill is in the kill!"

This went on for about ten seconds as Dorothy ran through the mob over to Brawner and gave him a big hug. He blushed. "Like we would ever let a lost girl disappear from our sights," he said, smiling.

He then turned to the dwarves. "Okay, okay, you dwarves. That's enough of your caterwauling. Now, let's see if they really wanna die in this tavern tonight."

Dunn looked at the eyes of the dwarves, sharp, clear, and hungry. He realized it would be a losing fight.

"Well, I never liked this tavern anyway..." he mumbled as he made his way out, past the dwarves. His men followed amidst jeers from the dwarves.

"How did you find me?" Dorothy asked.

"We followed your machine's tracks. A good thing, too. Several of the witch's men were following you as well... But they found our hammers and axes very painful."

"Why did you follow me?"

"We're not going to leave you with that scareman... We thought there would be trouble. We thought he had captured you, destroyed your machine, and took you to the witch."

"Oh no, he has been a perfect gentleman," Dorothy said. "He even helped free Achilles."

The scareman gave a grin, looked at the dwarves, and smiled. "A perfect gentleman," he said proudly.

"Bah, liar," Brawner said. "We are watching you, Scareman."

He then saw Leo and Achilles. "You have a strange taste in friends, my dear."

"Oh yeah, well... I never was very normal. Back home, most of my friends were not exactly normal, or cool. Kinda the weirdos and nerds, I guess."

"Bah, dwarves are often considered weird, but I have no idea of being a nerd," he said, smiling.

Brawner then walked over to Achilles and looked him up and down.

"Achilles, you look well."

"Yes, so do you, old warrior. I am doing fine now that Dorothy has freed me from my rusted tomb."

Brawner gave a wink to Achilles and tapped his chest with a knock. "We forged that iron from our home. No one builds armor like the dwarves of the Iron Mountains." He then turned to Leo. "So, no more leading from your throne, your Majesty?" the dwarf asked.

"I have made mistakes. That is true. My blade is eager for redemption, however," Leo said. He lowered his head.

"Yes, and not joining us was one of them. We really could have used you and your clan that day," the dwarven chieftain added.

"I was wrong. I have paid for my sins," Leo stated.

"I heard of the fall of the Isle of the Lions, the slavery and your battles in the queen's arena... I was enslaved as well."

"A true king admits his failures and attempts to redeem himself. I made a great error. I hope you will forgive me and tell your people my arrogance is much regretted."

The scareman whispered to Dorothy, "He has never claimed his mistakes... He must be truly sorry."

"The dwarves and lions have always been kin until that day; warriors who hunt and stories of battles were of legends. I was heartbroken when we entered the battle without you and your people. You hurt us deeply, your Highness. Your grandfather and I had killed dragons in our youth... dragons!" Brawner shouted.

Leo kneeled down and placed his pawlike hand on Brawner's war hammer. "I failed my people and our brothers, the dwarves of the Iron Mountains. I swear on my life I will never let you down again."

Brawner then kneeled and placed his small, thick hand on Leo's paw. "We are battle-bound and brothers of blood until the grave."

Leo stood up and helped the old dwarf to his feet. "I prayed you and your people would forgive me, though I did not deserve it. I was a fool," the lion king said.

"Maybe we have all been fools in our past, but not tonight." Brawner looked around the room.

"Take a table, and we will see if there is enough ale in this human-built shack!"

Killian looked at the commotion and shook his head. "Dwarves," he mumbled, "...and they're thirsty."

He signaled to his barkeep to go in the back. He then returned with a barrel of ale.

"Well, we have much to discuss," Killian said to Achilles. "And I think we will be up for several hours, so we might as well get settled."

"Agreed," Achilles said.

The scareman felt the negativity from the dwarves and found a table in the corner. He sat down, put Dorothy's backpack on the table, and began to look through one of her textbooks but then seconds later closed it and opened one of the hunting girl bikini magazines Dorothy had given him.

"Dorothy, if you want, there is a room upstairs and to your left... you can rest there," Killian said.

"Thank you... Oh, where is the restroom?"

"You can rest fine in that room; the bed is firm and very comfortable," Killian replied.

"I see," Dorothy said. "Okay... Um, well, I will retire to my room. Thanks again. I guess I'll see you all in the morning."

"Rest well," Achilles said.

Dorothy said goodnight to Leo and the scareman and then made her way up to her room as the dwarves drank, and their laughter became louder.

She entered the room with Conan at her side and saw the bed in the corner—a mattress stuffed with hay and feathers. She closed the door, and it muffled the noise from downstairs. She took out her cell phone, and it was 1:00 a.m. according to her time back home. At least the clock worked. She had 54% battery. She walked to the bed, kicked off her sneakers, and collapsed into it. Conan circled a couple of times and lay down next to the bed. She closed her eyes and within seconds was fast asleep.

# CHAPTER 15

## "IS COFFEE GOOD FOR A HANGOVER"

Dorothy rolled her head as she could feel warm breath push against her face, followed by the whimper of Conan. She pushed her head back into the pillow and tightened her eyes closed, trying to avoid the inevitable. Conan realized she had woken, however, and began to lick her face.

*So much for ten more minutes of sleep.*

Dorothy rolled over with a groan to pet her slobbering alarm clock of a dog. Opening her eyes just a bit she looked at the darkness of the room. "What happened, boy? Did the power go out? Where is my alarm clock?"

She then rolled over and tightened the blankets around her. "Oh well," she mumbled. "It can't be that early. The sun's still not out. Man, what a weird dream." Conan then took it upon himself to whimper louder and headbutt her with his cold, wet nose gently.

"I'll walk you later," Dorothy said. "I'm so tired."

Conan turned from the bed and walked away.

"Good boy," Dorothy whispered, and then she got comfortable, ready to get some more sleep.

Just as she was dozing off, a quick pounding came on the door of her room. She rolled over and sat up. She opened her eyes again and looked around the room, trying to make out the room's appearance in the limited light from cracks in what looked to be wooden shutters.

"Dorothy, it's me, Leo!" came a strong voice.

"Leo?" Dorothy asked herself. "I don't know any Leo."

"Yes, can I come in? I have great news."

"Leo?" she then whispered. "Who the hell is Leo?" She rocked out of bed and put her feet on the cold wood floor. "Wait a minute, where's the carpet? Where am I?"

She then stumbled to the door and felt for a doorknob.

"Dorothy, are you okay?" the voice asked.

*Was I drinking last night?* she thought to herself. "Hold on," she said and slowly opened the door.

Conan was next to her as she opened the door just a crack and peeked out. What she saw was a muscular manlike figure in shining armor and red boots. As she looked up, she saw a head resembling that of a lion. His hair appeared a golden mane. In a panic, she quickly slammed the door and fell against it to brace it shut.

"Oh my God!" she whispered.

"Dorothy, what's wrong?" came the voice once more. "Are you alright?"

"Um... wait a second!" Dorothy said with a quivering voice as she ran to the window. She threw open the wooden shutters and looked out. The sky was gray, the land was barren except for several small clusters that looked like fields of green, and mountains could be seen miles away.

"It wasn't a dream. Oh, man... I cannot believe this!" She quickly slipped her sneakers on. "How long have I been here? What about my aunt and schoolwork? What about Bob? Wait, Bob was cheating on me. It was not a dream! I gotta get some answers." She tied her sneakers and opened the door to the visitor. "Good morning!" she said, a little angry. "Let's go find that damn book. I wanna get home."

"That's what I came to tell you. The dwarves are going to travel with us!"

"Oh, that's great," Dorothy said with a concerned look. "Where are the others? And what time is it?"

"Oh, it's nearly noon... but I have to warn you it got pretty messy last night, drunken dwarves and all," Leo said, smiling.

"I'm sure. Come on," Dorothy said reluctantly.

She grabbed her backpack and cell phone from a small wooden table. She unplugged the power pack and looked at her phone. It was back to 81%. She looked at the charger, and it was flashing red. She shook her head angrily, grunted, and walked quickly past Leo, with Conan lagging behind. They walked down the stairs to the tavern as several dwarves lay scattered and snoring. The smell was that of a frat house after a wild party combined with a nursing home. She shuddered. She walked past the night of debauchery and opened the front door as Leo followed.

"Where are the scareman and Achilles?" she said angrily as she looked down the street.

"Oh, they're with Killian. They went to get more hungry plants and supplies for the tavern."

Then Dorothy spotted a well and walked over to it. She began to turn a crank that raised a rope, delivering water in a bucket.

She then took the bucket and splashed water on her face several times. Dorothy then turned to Leo and looked at him. "You know, I thought this was all just a dream, but it appears I have to go find some witch and retrieve a spell book just to get home. Oh, and try to stay alive... from whatever this godforsaken land of the resurrected dead, creatures, and people high on pot has to throw at me."

"Hey, you need to relax. We got a plan. You need some of that hungry plant... it will calm you down," the lion king said.

"No. I just need to get focused... Let's go back to the tavern. Maybe I can get some breakfast and try to figure this whole mess out."

The two walked back to the tavern as Dorothy kept her head down, looking at the ground, mumbling, and shaking her head. Leo went to put his thick paw hand on her shoulder but pulled it back. Now was not the time, and an angry, hungry woman is more aggressive than any lion.

# CHAPTER 16

## "BRAINS NOT BRAWN"

Dorothy had just finished a breakfast of eggs and bread as Killian and her companions returned. Leo sat at a nearby table sharpening his sword, humming a song, and the dwarves were slowly getting up and staggering right into the kitchen in the back of the tavern.

"Good, you're awake," Killian said. "We have a great deal to discuss."

Dorothy looked puzzled. "What is there to discuss? I'm just going to get that book and get home."

"It isn't going to be that easy, Dorothy," the scareman said. "Her castle is a fortress full of the resurrected dead and the Necro Lord's creatures. Though not at full strength during the day, they are still very strong."

"And let's not forget the trees," Achilles noted.

"Oh, yes, let's not forget those damn trees that rip people in half," Dorothy said. "I almost forgot." She opened the backpack and took out an energy drink. She popped the lid and chugged it. They all stared in awe. She slammed the empty energy drink. "So what you're telling me is we cannot just sneak in and get the book."

"Well, no... but with enough diversions, we could possibly attempt to sneak in and retrieve it," Achilles said. "We need a plan."

"That's where I come in. I am the smartest in the land," the scareman said confidently.

"When you're not forgetting spells..." Dorothy said angrily.

"I think we should have let her sleep some more," Leo grunted.

The scareman let out a sigh. "Dorothy, if I can retrieve my book... I may be able to stop the witch as well. I cannot kill her, but maybe this shotgun or that handheld gun could."

Dorothy shook her head and let out a sigh. "So now you want me to sneak into a fortress and blow some woman away with a shotgun? What about just getting the book and getting out?"

Killian laughed. "You, little lady, have a lot to learn about this world."

"Yeah, I know, but I thought we could just sneak in, get the book, and sneak out. Stitch-face does a spell, boom, you guys kill the witch, and I go home to a crappy life with a cheating fiancé and an aunt about to lose everything due to a woman at a bank that wants to take everything from our family."

Dorothy's head sank, and she covered her face with her hands.

Leo made his way over to the table and sat next to Dorothy. "Listen, Dorothy, this is the best time to strike. We can get more humans and dwarves, and catch her Bitchness off guard, and maybe if we're lucky we can kill her, get the book, and break the curse she put on the entire land."

"We have the tools and abilities to catch her unaware... I believe we really could do this with my magic," the scareman said.

Achilles laughed.

The scareman shot a look at Achilles but continued, "Leo's warrior spirit and a leader like Achilles, we could end her reign of power."

"And don't be forgetting the wee people who came to save your sorry butts!" came the gruff voice of Brawner.

He then took a seat next to Leo and smiled, his mouth half full of bread.

Killian shook his head, knowing his kitchen would be a disaster, and watched as more dwarves poured out and pots clanged. "I may be able to raise nearly fifty men to aid us," he said.

"I'll send some of my brothers this hour to our home to get as many that will fight," Brawner said. "We could get them all here within a day if we can also get the horses. The mountain dwarves are too far, but Orff's clan would be glad to slay evil creatures and trees."

Dorothy, seeing how she was outnumbered, looked at the faces of her newfound friends and folded her hands on the table.

"Well, Dorothy?" Leo asked.

"Okay," she said. "We all want something, so we have a common goal, but it had better be one hell of a plan."

The table cheered, and Dorothy felt several hands on her shoulders in agreement to her agreement. The team was united. Now, they just had to figure out the details.

"Well then, Achilles, our fearless leader, we need a great plan, and Scareman, you know the layout of the castle better than any of us," Leo said.

"Yes, we need to use our knowledge as a weapon against her if we are to stand a chance of victory," Achilles said.

"See, if you guys would get along for just five minutes, you could do anything. And if I could get rid of my headache, and my hatred and anger of being here, just think what we could do," Dorothy said, her smirk followed by a sigh.

"Save the hatred for the witch," Leo said. "Sometimes you have to get really angry and really dig deep to kill an enemy."

"Yes, I know. Feed the dark side..." she mumbled.

"Yes, yes, feed it, but control it," Leo said. "It's okay to go dark if you have to feed the hate, get angry, keep swinging until they stop moving."

"Oh, you would not like the stories we have back home. They do not push the dark side as good. You work for the light and maintain control at all times."

"Well, then you die. I do not care of such stories," Leo said. "I just want to win, and I will kill anything that keeps me from it."

"Yeah, you are definitely rated M for Mature. Now let's get this plan going and free this world and get me home," Dorothy said.

Suddenly Dorothy's phone buzzed. She pulled it out, and it spoke. "Kill the witch and save the world!" She looked down at the ad.

"Even your little machine is with us!" Achilles said. Another cheer came from the group.

"I keep forgetting to delete that game," Dorothy mumbled and looked at the screen. She went to delete it, but slid it to low power instead.

Brawner sent his dwarven messengers out, and Killian brought paper and ink to the table.

"We will need a lot of archers and fire to divert the trees," Achilles said. "And we must attack early in the morning, as the demons are weak in the morning. The powers of darkness are strongest under the moon's light and without rain this time, we can really cause some chaos."

"It will be hard to sneak into her domain with night so close. I'm sure there will be spies in the woods and rocks," the scareman said.

"Well, we cannot attack at night. She is too strong," answered Achilles.

"But what about the element of surprise?" Leo said. "If we're fast enough..."

"True, there is so much to consider. We have our work cut out for us. I would also assume she is on to us after last night. Word may have reached her already," the scareman said. "We must act quickly and keep her off guard."

The group sat around the table talking amongst themselves, at some points arguing, and others agreeing that only the perfect plan could work and end the witch's reign.

# CHAPTER 17

## "THE CALM BEFORE THE STORM"

The plan was finished in the late afternoon, and through much fighting and yelling, the group had decided on what would be the best way to surprise the witch and her demonic army.

Dorothy had left the city walls to clear her head. She walked only a few yards from the walls to get away from the noisy, but lovable, dwarves. Conan was with her. He walked playfully alongside as she walked past the Diamond City. She looked out over the barren land and just sighed.

"I don't know if we can do this, Conan... I mean save a world. I'm just some girl from a small town... kinda ironic, I guess. It always works on TV or in a movie, but something does not feel right. I mean, who am I? Girl power, right? This is not going to college or winning some competition, though. This is life and death, and it's not even my life. It's theirs, but if I want even my crappy life back, I have to do this, don't I? I do not want to shoot anyone unless absolutely necessary. This is crazy. This is just crazy."

"Dorothy!" a voice yelled. She turned and saw Leo, Achilles, and the scareman running to meet her.

"We thought we should spend our time with you before the battle," Leo said, smiling. "We may not see each other again."

"That's horrible," she said with a laugh. "Are you always so blunt?"

"Well, it is true," the scareman said. "Many have died in our world... so we wanted to thank you and spend what little time we may have left with you."

"If we fail, the witch will surely kill all of us and any others in hiding... so we have to win this. We must retrieve the book. I know I can come back to lead us to victory," Achilles said.

"Well, I'm not too worried. Our plan is very good, and we know her weaknesses... so we just have to use them against her," Dorothy noted.

"Yes, tomorrow will be a great day indeed!" Leo roared with excitement. "Glory again, or glory in death!"

Dorothy pulled out her cell phone and set it to camera.

"Okay, if we're going to make history, then we need to capture this moment forever. My battery is low, but a few pictures should be fine, I hope."

"That little box can make history?" Achilles asked.

"Just stand closer."

They huddled together, and Dorothy held the phone up.

"We call this a selfie... People do this in my world all the time."

They saw themselves in the small camera's case.

"It's like a magic mirror!" the scareman said.

"I am pretty good-looking," Leo stated and moved his hair with his hand.

"Achilles, you need to bend down. It's cutting off your head."

"Cutting off my head?" he snorted angrily.

"No, just squat down," Dorothy said. The giant iron general crunched down.

"Say cheese!"

"Cheese?" the scareman asked. "Is that a magic word for machines?"

Dorothy sighed and smiled. "Just say cheese!"

They all said, "cheese," and Dorothy snapped the picture. She spun the phone around and showed them.

They all stared at it in appreciative silence.

"I would take more, but the battery is low, and my spare case is low, too."

The scareman touched the screen with his gloved hand.

"It's beautiful. Look at us; we're all there."

"We look very powerful," Leo noted.

"It's a great picture," Dorothy said. "In my world, we send pictures and moving pictures to each other on our phones."

"That's amazing!" the scareman said. "You could send spells and information!"

"Yep, these things and the Internet changed our world in just a few years. Technology is not all bad, Stitch-face."

"I guess not," the scareman said. "But what of magic?"

"If we had magic, we abused it and lost it thousands of years ago. But it was not technology that killed it, but greed and power. It's a long story, and I do not even know how to explain it for now."

The travelers then began to walk out into the field of hungry plants.

"After we save our world, I would like to return to the Land of the Lion and rebuild our islands. I was not the leader I should have been," Leo said with a tone of regret.

"I think I will try to build a new group of soldiers to represent humans, dwarves, and our newfound unified peace. Maybe even construct a machine like Dorothy's. That Ford was very useful," Achilles noted.

"What about you, Stitch-face?" Dorothy asked.

"I'm not sure if I can become a man again... I may just retire to the Magic Mountain and maybe heal people. Being so hurt and having hurt so many... I need to mend and make people feel better. Yes, I think that's what I will do."

"What will you do when we get you home, Dorothy?" Achilles asked.

"Well, I can't sell Bob's truck. The trees destroyed it. So we will not have the money to save our family's business. It's like a tavern: great food and grand company. We owe too much money to the bank so... I guess I will finish school and try to start over again. It seems like I always have to start over from the bottom, and no matter what I do or try, I fail. I do not have a lot of friends... I never did," she said, as her voice quivered a bit.

"Well, maybe that's what you need," Leo said. "A better and stronger circle of warriors!"

"Yeah, that is something I can definitely do when I do get home," Dorothy said with renewed optimism.

"I think all this excitement has my mind racing... I remember spells and things I thought I had lost... but a lot is coming back!" the scareman said. "Reading your schoolbooks rekindled some things, I believe!"

"Just like riding a bike, huh?" Dorothy said.

"A what?" The scareman gave a curious look.

"Never mind," Dorothy said, smiling.

Leo then stopped and looked around the field. He gave a quick sniff of the air.

"What is it, friend?" Achilles asked.

Leo looked confused. "Well, it's nothing... I thought I could smell a faint scent of enemies in the air, but night is hours away."

"Maybe it's the scent of the dead ones that lingers from the woods caught on a strong wind..." the scareman said.

"Maybe, but I smelled no rotting corpses, just resurrected warriors."

"There is no way night creatures could come out during the day," the scareman said. "The resurrected warriors hunt by night," the scareman suggested.

Leo sniffed the air again.

"It is from the east, the witch's domain," he said, and the group looked toward the woods. "We should get back," the scareman said. "Just in case."

"Scareman is right," Achilles said. "Let's head back." They turned to leave the entrance of the Diamond City when Leo shouted, "Creatures!"

They turned and looked as several black dots appeared over the forest and began to approach.

"What witchcraft is this?!" the scareman shouted. "It's that damn book. I bet she found a spell for them!"

"It isn't possible," Leo stated.

"Anything is possible when dealing with her," the scareman shouted with great concern in his voice. "Let's get back behind the walls of the city!"

The group began to run back through the field. As they looked back, the witch's evil creatures began to swoop ever closer.

"We have to fight them!" Leo said. "We're never gonna make it otherwise!"

"No!" Achilles shouted. "I'll try to slow them down... They cannot kill me, and I'm too heavy for them to fly with!"

Dorothy looked at Leo. "What do we do?"

"Do as he says. Achilles will fight with the fury of a thousand humans!"

Achilles stood his ground, raised his axe in anticipation, and stood firm as his friends hurried ahead. They began to slow down soon, however, as they began to tire.

"Damn, I'm out of shape!" Dorothy said as her pace slowed.

The scareman then began chanting and raised his arms as they fled. A blue wave of light rippled around them as they ran, and suddenly Dorothy felt a boost in confidence… as if she were invincible, and also a renewed breath in her lungs. Leo also smiled as his lungs breathed easier as they continued to run.

"Nice touch!" Leo said to the scareman.

"I told you it's coming back to me!" he boasted. "I just need more time…"

The creatures were now just yards from Achilles and began their dive. The brave iron general raised his axe and readied to meet them in combat.

"Come on, you demon bastards!" he screamed.

Suddenly they pulled up and flew over his head… He watched as they blew by him and went sailing off toward his companions.

"No!" he screamed. "Fight me, you cowards!" He ran as quickly as his iron body allowed as steam poured from his neck.

Dorothy turned around and looked back as the flying creatures approached. "We're not going to make it!"

Leo turned and braced himself for a fight. He pulled his sword and began to run toward the pack of demons.

"Wizard, they must want Dorothy! Get her to the city. I'll do what I can," he yelled.

The scareman grabbed Dorothy's hand, and, mumbling another spell, the two comrades in arms ran even faster to the city gates.

Leo leaped high into the air and savagely grabbed two creatures, bringing them to the ground. He swung his blade and went to cut off their heads. He stopped and turned his attention to the helmets that covered their eyes. Achilles sprinted up from behind and, using his axe, smashed one of the creatures in the chest, pouring black blood all over Leo, who himself cut off the head of the other creature.

"Come on!" Leo screamed, and the two ran as fast as they could toward the rest of the creatures who were closing in on Dorothy and the scareman at a rapid pace.

Dorothy looked ahead as the city gates sat only thirty yards ahead of them. "We're not gonna make it!" she yelled as the flapping of dozens of wings pounded behind her, growing ever closer and closer.

The creatures suddenly flew by Dorothy and the scareman. They landed and encircled them with a devilish grin.

"Now what?!" Dorothy yelled.

The scareman looked as Leo and Achilles charged toward their stranded friends.

"We just have to stall them until they get here," said Dorothy. "Damn it! Where is the shotgun..."

"I went for a walk. I didn't bring it with me, for crying out loud. I have the pistol, however!"

"Well, use that. Or better yet, cast a spell with all your might!"

Conan barked and lunged at the closest creature, who backed off.

"Cast a spell or something! Come on!"

"I'm working on it. Hold on!" the scareman shouted.

Leo was just yards away. The brave lion king screamed out, "The helmets! Remove their helmets! They are magic!"

The creatures grew in confidence and began to tighten their circle of destruction and evil.

"Okay, I have one!" the scareman said and began to mumble. Without warning, however, three creatures swooped from the air and grabbed Dorothy by the shoulders. They lifted her up into the air.

"They have her!" Leo yelled and pursued even harder. Achilles raised his left arm, and taking aim, fired three darts that flew through the air and struck one of the dastardly creatures.

The scareman grabbed hold of Dorothy and tried to fight off the creatures who lifted him as well. Dorothy felt her feet leave the ground and screamed as the helmeted creatures lifted her into the air. The remaining creatures assaulted the scareman and began to rip his body apart. He fought back but with little chance, as one of his arms was torn off. Leo ran into the fray and began slamming his sword into the helmets of the creatures who, facing Leo's fierce attack, left the scareman and attacked Leo as Dorothy was lifted into the air.

"Achilles!" Dorothy screamed. The iron general hurled his axe, which impaled itself in the back of one of Dorothy's captors, who fell to the ground with a satisfying thud.

The two remaining creatures flew ever swifter carrying Dorothy, whose demise seemed certain. Conan pursued and savagely barked at Dorothy's captors, bravely lunging toward them. Leo met with Achilles in the center of battle as creatures fought them on the ground.

"No!" Achilles screamed.

The evil creatures and their captive swiftly disappeared over the fields and forest as the two warriors left a trail of black blood strewn around the field of hungry plants.

Leo placed his hand on Achilles's hulking shoulder. "What could we have done? She uses magic we cannot counter. We must stick to the plan and not let Dorothy's demise make us stray from our mission."

The iron general spun around. "She is not dead yet! The witch will torture her until she reveals our plans. We have to move in and save her!"

"You know she will be killed without mercy; can't you just look at things rationally? We have to stick with our plan if we are to save the world! Dorothy is gone, but we live..."

"Always focusing on yourself, aren't you, lion king? You're a selfish coward. Damn you!"

Achilles stormed off to find the scareman.

"I am not a coward... I am the bravest creature in our world!" Leo shouted.

"Yes, only when you have something to gain. Dorothy saved me, and I will save her, with or without you!"

Leo ran behind Achilles. "You cannot save her... and what about the plan?"

"You said the element of surprise, so be it! I'm gonna surprise her Wickedness... We will attack early before she can get our plan from Dorothy."

"A night attack is suicide, Achilles... Have you got rust in your head?"

"I will not leave her to die. She brought us together and gave us hope; fight with us or walk away like you did in the Ten Days of Darkness."

The iron general then began sifting through the plants, looking for the scareman. Conan stood yards away, barking as his owner disappeared into the gray sky. Leo growled and watched as the iron general picked up the dazed scareman. Achilles felt around and picked up the scareman's straw arm and walked slowly to the city gates as humans and dwarves ran to greet them.

"Achilles. I'm sorry. I could not... I could not think of a spell quickly enough! I will be okay. I can heal myself, then I will help you rescue Dorothy," the scareman said.

"Good, 'cause I have a witch to carve up," he said, and the ground shook as Achilles stormed back toward the city gates.

The two entered the city as Leo stood outside, looking at the gray skies and wondering about how the rebellion was all but doomed.

# CHAPTER 18

## "BREAKING THE SPRIRIT"

Dorothy's head pounded. She tried to open her eyes, but they felt welded shut. She let out a weak sigh. She then went to rub her head and heard a metal clang. She forced her eyes open and discovered her hands were chained to a wall. She stood up from the cold floor and looked around at what appeared to be a holding cell. There was a small window to her left and several shelves and books randomly scattered around the room.

The only door was several feet across from her. It was her only freedom from this library from hell. She remembered being ripped off the ground at the Diamond City and then as she was being raised into the air she had passed out. She was not too fond of heights. She looked around the room again and saw her small pocketbook spilled out on a wooden table and her pistol, too. She tried to squeeze her hands from the chains, but it was no good.

"Great," she mumbled.

As if on cue, the wooden door creaked open. The first to enter was the Necro Lord. He glided in as if hovering; then several resurrected soldiers staggered and limped behind him. Their foul stench filled the room quickly, and Dorothy turned her head, hoping to not sniff any more than she had to. After the Necro Lord and his band of bodyguards had positioned themselves, a huge ape-like demon walked in, never breaking eye contact with Dorothy. She began to squirm.

The witch then strolled in. Her dark eyes gleamed, and her thin, pale lips turned into a twisted smile. Her gown was long, black and had crushed velvet trim around the neck and arms. She let out a light chuckle. "Well, it seems our little guest of honor is awake."

Dorothy looked at the gun on the table again. The gunpowder could be put to use. *Maybe...*

"I do not know what you have been told about our world, young lady, but I can assure you, you have been lied to."

The witch walked up to Dorothy and quickly grabbed her by the cheek.

"We have a saying here, 'Never anger the witch,' and you, little girl, have done that."

The witch dropped her hand from Dorothy's cheeks but returned it with a slap across her young face. Dorothy's eyes burned, and she immediately screamed out, looking into the witch's eyes. She wasn't afraid. Oh, no, she was pissed off.

"Well, it looks like you have a bit of fire in you after all." The witch then smacked Dorothy again. This time, blood dripped from Dorothy's lips. Dorothy spat in the witch's face.

The witch laughed. "You do not know anything about the horror I will do to you for that show of disrespect," she said as she wiped the blood and spit from her eyes and cheek.

"Just let me go. I want to go home. I do not even want to be in your shitty world!" Dorothy yelled as she thrashed her chains again.

The witch then grabbed her by the jaw and slammed her back into the stone wall, pinning her with incredible strength. Dorothy let out a small whimper. The witch looked down at her pale hand and noticed the blood.

"Blood Lust!" she summoned. The giant demon ape immediately strode forward and stood next to his queen. She slowly caressed his face with her bloody hand. He let out a growl of pleasure. Dorothy looked in horror as the beast sniffed and then kissed the witch's hand, attempting to taste the drying blood.

"It seems she bleeds like anyone. This visitor or so-called savior I have heard about is just a mere mortal girl after all. Why so many would help someone just as weak as themselves is beyond my comprehension," the witch said.

Blood Lust let out a small chuckle. "Indeed, my Queen. In fact, it is not even virgin blood."

"Well, I guess we cannot sacrifice her then, can we?" the witch said, glancing over to the Necro Lord.

"Blood is blood... I can use her," he bellowed.

"Screw you, asshole!" Dorothy yelled in defiance.

The beast stepped up and snorted, his hot and stale breath on Dorothy's face.

"No." The witch lightened her grip as Dorothy regained her footing. "We have too many things we need to know before we change her." Blood Lust stepped away in anger. The witch then let go of Dorothy and walked over to the table. Her hand grazed over Dorothy's purse.

"What I want to know is of your magic, your world. Were you sent here as a spy?"

"That's just my stuff, and I am not a spy. Listen, I just want to get home!"

"And where is home? Maybe we can make an arrangement," the witch asked with an evil grin.

"You're not going to believe me anyway," Dorothy said.

"Just tell me why you are here, why you helped the dwarves, and why you freed Achilles!" The witch was losing her patience.

"I just did what was right and ethical. Listen, if you can get me home, maybe things will get back to normal if I leave..." Dorothy said temptingly.

"You are not leaving or going home. You will stay with me and tell me everything I need to know. I have already found out several things about you from my spies and my trees. Make it easier on yourself and tell me what I demand, and maybe I will kill you and your friends quickly."

"I am not a spy!"

Suddenly Dorothy's phone began to vibrate. The witch ran over to it and picked it up. She touched the screen.

"Kill the witch and save the world!" it chimed.

She watched the screen as a woman with huge breasts in a white dress holding a scepter danced rhythmically.

"Kill the witch," it said again.

The witch's eyes grew large. "You evil creature! Your small magic mirror is feeding you orders!"

"No, it's a game. It's an app for a game!"

The witch slammed the phone down and stormed over to Dorothy.

"This is not a game, you spy! That small magic machine told me of your plans. How many are in your army?!"

"I do not have an army. I am Dorothy from Kansas! I do not have magic or a machine... Sweet Jesus, woman... I just want to go home!"

The witch slapped her again.

Dorothy could see she wasn't getting anywhere, but was thinking about how much the witch already knew. She had to hope she could be rescued, or at least try to free herself later.

*If she thinks I have magic, then I will act like I do,* Dorothy thought. "Fine! You want to see my magic? Why I am here?"

The witch was intrigued by Dorothy's sudden turn in attitude. "Yes, I do, and I will learn them and use them to destroy the rest of those who oppose me. Now talk!"

Dorothy looked at the pistol and then nodded at it. "See that? That is most of my power. If you hand it to me, I will show you how to use it."

The witch smiled and picked up the gun. "Tell you what, you tell me how, my dear... I am no fool."

"It's called a horoscope... It enables you to see into the future and even see other worlds."

The witch held it by the handle and looked carefully at it. "Other worlds?" she mumbled.

"Yes, that's where I am from. Another world. First, you have to hold it with the end between your eyes and look down the long barrel end."

"What kind of worlds?" the witch said as she looked over Dorothy carefully. "How do I know it's not a weapon?"

"Look, you said you wanted to see my magic, and I am trying to tell you what I can. Why would I lie to you? I am chained to a wall, surrounded by your soldiers. The last thing I need to do is trick you!"

The witch smiled. "You are no foolish girl. I can see that. But what other worlds? Will I see your world? Can I use this as a weapon?"

"It has several uses. First, you place it between your eyes and look down the barrel, and then pull the lever back. That is what activates the magic powers within."

The witch was not convinced.

She handed the gun to Blood Lust.

"In case there is a trap in the other world or a curse, I need your great strength to fight it."

"Yes, my Queen," Blood Lust replied. He stood in front of the queen and raised the gun upside down with the barrel pointing between his beady eyes. The witch stood over his shoulder and pressed down the barrel as well, with one eye on her captive.

"It's a bright light. That's the portal. There will be a pop sound; then you will see the light," Dorothy said.

She realized the witch wouldn't fall for it, but at least she would take out Blood Lust.

Blood Lust looked down the barrel, and his thick dark finger quivered as he found the triggering device, awaiting the magic. The clawlike finger slowly pulled the trigger back. There was a loud blast, and blood sprayed all over the witch.

Blood Lust stumbled back and fell on top of his queen. The gun fell to the floor just feet from Dorothy. The Necro Lord hovered to his queen. The witch, in a rage, pushed the heavy bloody body off her and wiped the blood from her pale face. She looked up at Dorothy and then down at Blood Lust, who shook and twitched. Blood poured from his head. There was little left of his skull and brain. The queen lunged at Dorothy, who had a hopeful smile on her face. This faded into fear as a blade was placed on her throat. The witch looked deep into Dorothy's eyes. Dorothy had never seen such darkness before. It made her stomach twist, and she looked away.

"Listen, you little bitch, one more trick and I will feed you to the worms. Do you think I am a fool? Do you think I do not know of your attempt to retrieve the book or your plans to attack the castle? I know all, my dear. And the few things I may not know I will know by nightfall!"

The witch then took the blade and cut Dorothy across the cheek. She raised the blade and licked its tip. "Do not think you will live long here. For once I have my answers, you and your dear friends will all be dead, and your skeletons will be hanging on my castle walls."

The witch turned and looked at the body of the dead beast. "I will take him back to my lair. I may be able to revive him. Bring him!" the Necro Lord said.

The witch stormed out with her troops behind her. Dorothy saw the door slam shut and looked down at the blood puddle on the floor and then out the dreary window to the land that lay under the witch's curse. She sniffled, and tears ran down her cheeks. Home was too far from her now, and with the witch knowing all of their plans, she would soon die as would her new dear friends. She then sat back on the floor and began to sob, the tears burning into her cut face.

She just wanted to go home.

# CHAPTER 19

## "CHAOS! CHAOS! CHAOS!"

Despair fell on the faces of the men and dwarves as the news of Dorothy's capture and the creatures' attack that took place spread around the city. Many grumbled and claimed they would not fight the witch and her evil army. The people and dwarves knew one thing, however, the witch would attack them immediately simply because of the threat of a rebellion. It was a stalemate however one looked at it.

Inside the dimly lit Lucky Lady Tavern, Achilles, Leo, the scareman, dwarves and a handfull of humans sat at a table looking at a piece of paper that at one time had been a plan of action and surprise, not possible now, however.

"We are still going to have to fight," Brawner began. "She will attack us and destroy the city."

"Well, it depends if she has tortured any information from Dorothy yet," Achilles noted.

"She will be dead by tomorrow's first light," Leo mumbled in despair.

The scareman gave Leo a look of anger, followed by the rest of the table.

"What? Think about it... she is as good as dead. I have seen the things the witch can do, and trust me, that girl is gonna break like a dead tree branch under the terrible torture the queen must be putting her through."

"Well, we have to find a way to rescue her then, and quick!" Achilles said. "Get her to safety and decide on a new plan. The witch would never suspect a direct assault on her castle..."

"That sounds too risky, even for me," Leo snorted.

"I think I could get a few of us into the castle," the scareman interjected. "But we would have to be small in number and have a distraction."

"We could be a distraction," Brawner said. "We would love to show the witch a good time..."

"Maybe a castle invasion at night?" the scareman added.

"Are you out of your straw-filled head?" Leo shouted. "Yes, let's attack her at her fortress when her powers are the strongest. That makes no sense whatsoever!"

"No... sneak in right before dawn, and in the heat of the confusion, a group finds Dorothy and gets her out," the scareman said.

"I don't know how many men would want to risk their hides for the rescue of a girl they don't know," Killian said.

"The witch will attack us soon anyway. I think we should try a peaceful attempt to get her confidence back," a man suggested. "I have a family to think about."

"Well, now I know you have smoked too much of the hungry plant," Leo said, laughing.

"This city is as good as dead. We have to fight or leave. Those are the choices we have," Achilles said.

The small band of warriors sat very quietly. Was it worth the life of this newcomer to their world, or would another chance of freedom slide through their fingers like the muddy soil of their land?

There was a cough.

Then a grin from Brawner.

Then a dark chuckle.

Achilles knew that look. It was of hungry, war-filled eagerness that all dwarves mustered in their souls. They began to stomp their feet. They would welcome death on a battlefield over to be slaves once again. The iron general stood up.

"I will fight to save Dorothy and find any way to free the land from the witch and her evil hordes," Achilles said with confidence. "I will lead us to war and victory!"

The dwarves screamed with glee. The scareman nodded his agreement. Killian raised his sword high in the air. "My blade will join you and your quest."

The dwarves cheered again. Leo sat with his arms folded, looking at the scareman and Achilles in defiance.

"A mad plan... This is suicide and madness. Besides, I believe she will be dead by dawn."

"Then we will free her this night," the scareman said. "I can get us into the castle... I know magic that can get us in. If I find my book, I can help send Dorothy home and kill the witch. She would never see us coming into her domain."

After several seconds, the proud lion king could not hold back.

"I will help, and I will die before I let her enslave me to her entertainment a second time."

The dwarves cheered again, and dozens of thick, stubby hands grabbed Leo and began shaking him with excitement.

"I agree with the scareman's idea if he is strong enough," Achilles boasted.

"Do not worry about me. I am still the greatest wizard of this land. Now hear this plan," the scareman said.

The band of fighters drew close together as the scareman began. "We must attack without warning and risk all. Divide her forces and give her ego the confusion of a lifetime."

## "ANYBODY HOME?"

Under the spotty, soft, warm glare of the double moons, the woods of the Forest of the Damned crawled with life. Night in these woods was not a time for the weak of heart or weak in body. Four figures dipped in and out of the treacherous shadows. They made no noise as they traveled on.

Achilles's swift axe led the small band, followed by Leo the Conquerer and the scareman who carried Dorothy's shotgun and wore her backpack. Behind the unseemly comrades was Dorothy's dog, Conan—sniffing every plant he could and watering them as well. Making their way to a small cluster of thorn bushes, the group saw their destination.

There, high on a rocky cliff, was a castle standing alone. There were no trees, shrubs, or rocks littering the landscape, providing cover, only earth and mud. Torchlight could be seen from afar, like stars lighting up the walls and battlements. Around the castle, there lay a great moat. A monstrous iron and wooden drawbridge lay over the pit that surrounded the dreadful castle of doom.

The adventurers stood fearlessly looking at the castle, knowing this night could be their last. They watched as several flying creatures hovered over the castle walls and then landed on the rooftops. Patrols of the resurrected dead staggered, looking for unwanted guests or a late-night snack of blood. There was a small path that led up to the castle from the woods. Its stone stairs were caked in mud and stained with blood. No one trod the steps to the witch's domain unless they were her own living dead. Life, however, began to leave the castle as several trees emerged through the hideous front gate. Their roots pushed their brittle gray bodies forward, with gaping jagged mouths open, and eyes burned black with hate. Behind the half a dozen trees, many resurrected soldiers followed in a drudgery walk as work had begun. Guard duty was not pleasant. Whether you were living or dead, everyone still had to work. The trees made their way down the steps and went toward the east side of the forest, good for the four heroes but bad for the creatures in the east end of the forest. The resurrected dead, close to a dozen, missing limbs and patches of skin waited in line along the drawbridge. They stood still as statues. The bodies of the soldiers would sway as the breeze would gently blow, and soft drops of rain fell from the cloudy sky.

"Well now, we have made it this far; what do you suppose we can do from here?" Leo whispered.

To save the girl and risk his own neck was unheard of. He was once a king; this was beneath him. His mind raced back to his days of glory and of his kingdom. Maybe this was how he would be remembered: killed saving a girl who died at the hands of the witch on a suicide mission with two other wanted traitors to the witch. His mind went blank for a second, and he heard his ego whisper, *If you pull this off, you're a god.* He stood up with a smirk.

"I believe I can get us into the castle with the proper spell," the scareman said confidently. "I just have to remember it."

Achilles paid little attention and scanned the area for more trouble. In his hand was his thunderous axe, and he yearned to throw its blade into the girth of the trees. The chainsaw was still in his thigh compartment. He liked it, but his axe was his closest ally.

The scareman stared into the night sky, mumbling under his breath. He would have to say the incantation just perfectly if they were to make it into the castle by his power.

"What is taking so damned long," Leo growled. His patience burned like a short fuse.

The wizard turned to his accomplices. "I believe I remember the spell of teleportation… now if you will join me over there."

"Well, it's about time," Leo whined.

The three warriors made their way to a clearing. The scareman took a stick from the ground and drew a circle in the mud and clay. "We cannot have any part of our bodies outside of this outline, or we cannot teleport." The adventurers stood facing one another as Conan stood next to the shotgun between them, wagging his stubby tail. The scareman threw up his hands and began chanting a deep and guttural language.

*"Tunock born cantis gannonan…"* he whispered again and again. He said this phrase over and over building its depth and volume until it became a shout. Wind blew in their faces, and lights appeared around them. The iron general stood stock still waiting for anything and trusting no magic. Leo watched in awe as the lights around him began to blind him. Conan let out a small whimper, and the scareman continued his chanting like a madman.

There was the crack of thunder, and suddenly the four of them were gone.

# CHAPTER 21

## "SURPRISE"

The blinding lights of magic quickly faded, and the eyes of the lion king focused. At first glance, everything was blurry, a swirl of colors, but within seconds Leo saw the faces of his comrades. They stood frozen for a brief moment realizing they were within the castle's walls! Achilles turned his iron skull to find the best possible view of their vantage for this surprise invasion. His eyes then stared in disbelief as he saw they were surrounded. Trees, the resurrected dead, and creatures stood with weapons drawn and pointed at the intruders. The creatures surrounding them made no sound, but their faces gave host to mockery. Conan let out a small whine, and the three warriors turned to face the onslaught of the enemy.

Leo slid his hand slowly on his sword's hilt and growled lightly. "Great work, Scareman. Any more spells in that straw-filled head? Maybe you could slit our throats in our sleep?" the lion king growled.

"This was not my plan," the scareman shot back as the enemy began to laugh and taunt with their blades at the ready.

Then came a shout!

At the top of the courtyard, a winding stairwell rose to a ledge, and there, standing like a goddess of eternal night, was the witch. She ran her hand across her cheek and smiled.

"It was my plan, fools. You have done well, Scareman. You promised me the rebels, and you have delivered."

Achilles turned to the scareman; his eyes blazed red. "You traitor!" he shouted as he then used his left hand to grab the scareman and hold him up high in the air. The shotgun fell from his soft grip, and he smiled at Achilles.

"You have sentenced us to death! The dwarves will die; Dorothy will die... and for that, you will die as well!"

The scareman let out a chuckle. "Oh, Achilles, do I look that much of a fool?"

Several trees made their way swiftly to the iron general and wrapped their branches around his mighty frame. The axe fell from his grip as he fought the vines and branches. Then the scareman fell from his grasp.

The witch closed her dark eyes and stepped off the high platform. Her body floated down like a feather. She opened her eyes and placed her hand out to the scareman, who took it eagerly. She helped him to his feet as Leo growled angrily.

"It would be wise to remove your hand from your blade, Lion King, though I could let you play with it in the arena once again..." the witch suggested with a laugh.

Leo complied reluctantly with the witch's orders. Achilles twitched and fought the grip of the trees, but quickly stopped, realizing it was futile. The scareman looked at the two captured heroes.

"You have to realize the situation. How could I side with a fallen general and the king of a dying race? I had but one choice," the scareman said. "The right choice. That girl cannot help us. She was doomed to fail!" the scareman said.

The witch smiled and looked at the lion king. "Your fans will be glad you have returned to me." She snapped her fingers as several resurrected dead surrounded Leo and Achilles. They carried heavy chains.

"Bind them, hands and feet. And use three times as many chains on Achilles, Black Root." The giant demon tree grunted and slithered over, ripping the mighty Sun Seeker from Achilles's iron grip. If a machine could ever feel pain, if a machine could ever cry, it would be at that very moment.

"No more chances to kill my trees," Black Root hissed.

The servants did as the witch commanded, and after much heckling, the two warriors stood imprisoned in their iron bonds. Achilles stared at the scareman, never looking away, never blinking.

"I am just a weak-minded old man, just a liar," he said to Achilles. "No more! She will make me human again. No more straw, no more mockery! I will rule this land with her!"

The scareman felt the eyes on him but ignored their cold stare. He then walked over to Leo. "It is better to live as a dog than die as a lion," the scareman grunted.

Leo, in a rage, thrashed and then spit at the scareman. "If I ever feel freedom again, I will rip you to bloody shreds!"

"I am not worried," the scareman said. He walked over to Black Root and ripped the giant axe Sun Seeker from his grip and hoisted it high. "I will keep this as a trophy, how I fooled the great General Achilles."

Achilles stared at the scareman, thinking about the trust he had lost and the lies he had believed. He had pledged his oath to Dorothy to protect her with all his might, and he had failed. He was fooled by the traitor, Scareman.

"Take them to the dungeon and keep them guarded. Scareman, please do the honors of escorting them. I want the arrival to their new home to be cheery, and if they try anything, I expect you to use that magic of yours to rip them apart."

The scareman bowed. "As you wish, my Queen."

The scareman picked up the shotgun and rested Sun Seeker across his frail shoulders. He struggled briefly but lifted his head high and smirked at the iron general one more time for good measure.

"And take that foul beast with you," the witch added as she pointed to Conan, who barked and jumped in deep confusion about what was going on around him.

The horde of resurrected dead and three creatures paraded the vanquished heroes out of the courtyard, down a set of stairs, and through a stone doorway. The heavy chains hung from the captives' bodies and dragged along the floor, producing a dark scratching melody as the scareman marched triumphantly behind the group.

# CHAPTER 22

## "CRUEL INTENTIONS"

The corridor reeked of despair. Torchlight and shadows were all that could be seen as the witch's troops pushed the fallen heroes on.

Achilles tried to piece together the last few minutes in his head, but could not. What did he do wrong? He would never see freedom again. His maker created him stronger than this. Dorothy freed him once, and for vengeance's sake, he had walked right into a trap. Now he understood why Leo had hidden and hunted in the woods, never trying to gain his vengeance. He had been a fool. He felt a cranking in his chest. He knew it was his heart.

He thought of Dorothy once more and let out a sigh.

Leo, with a scowl on his face, kept his head up as he felt prods in his back and heard laughing. He was still a king, and his ego would never let him forget it. He had escaped once, and he would do it again. A sharp spear dug into his shoulder, and he growled and looked over behind him, only to see the faces of the creatures mocking the once-proud king.

The prisoners were led down three flights of stone stairs and deep within a corridor. Several yards later, they arrived at the dungeon. It was a round room with several cells. Instruments of torture littered the floor. There were no other entrances to the horror chamber. Leo looked at the cells and saw that nothing in them moved. Death joined the despair in the air. A huge hairy beast sat at an iron desk, and as the prisoners approached, he sat up and grinned.

"Fresh meat?" he said. "Legendary, as well... most fantastic. Well, well, well. Gentlemen, let me introduce myself. My name is Clot. I am your new owner and giver of life. You will find I am unfair and vile. But if you do everything I say, you may live for another hour or so."

Leo ignored him; Achilles looked at the keys that hung from the dungeon master's belt.

"We have two rules here. One—I am in charge, and two—remember rule one. If you do not break here, I may send you to the arena to fight. If not, I'll leave you here to rot, as you can only look forward to a slow, painful, pathetic death."

Leo counted the number of guards. There were three creatures, seven resurrected dead, and the deceptive and cowardly Scareman. He could kill four or five, but no more than this. He looked down at his chains angrily.

"Enough of the pleasantries," Clot said and began to walk toward a large cell. "I believe it's time to make your-selves at home."

Leo and Achilles stood facing the cell as cheers began. The scareman walked up slowly between the spears and swords and placed his hands on the shoulders of his once loyal friends.

"In you go," he said.

Achilles looked over his shoulder and looked at the Scareman. "I should have killed you when I had the chance."

The scareman's face transformed from a smile to a grimace. Suddenly, Achilles heard the scareman's voice, but his lips did not move. *<On my command, your bonds will be like straw. Kill everything in this room... everything but Leo, the dog, and myself, understand?>*

"What? How are you? You're in my thoughts."

*<Just do it, you oversized iron bucket. Kill everything on my signal!>* Achilles looked at the scareman and then at Leo, who was smiling evilly at the cell's bars.

"Kill everything, Achilles," Leo said in a low growl.

The scareman slowly slid his hands down to Achilles's chains, and lightly touching them, he whispered just one word. Achilles felt the weight of the chains lift. The heckling once again started as the spears began to prod the captives once more. The scareman made his way to the back of the crowd.

Leo began to enter his cell when suddenly there was a shout.

"Now!" called out the scareman.

Achilles spun around, and his chains snapped like string. He thrashed out, knocking three of the resurrected dead to the floor. Only one managed a crawl, and then he too fell face down.

Chaos reigned.

Clot began to run toward a rope that hung from a bell in a desperate effort to sound the alarm. Leo ran from his cell in hopes of stopping him, but as swiftly as Clot reached for the rope, a sharp blast came from the scareman's shotgun. Clot fell with a thud to the dungeon floor.

"Resurrected idiots!" the scareman yelled and then tossed the great axe to Achilles, who took it from the air.

He began to thrash mercilessly through the air, killing another of the guards.

Leo nodded and ran toward the entrance of the dungeon to block any chance of escape. Even in chains, the lion king could be a vicious guard. Achilles made swift work of the last of the resurrected dead and sent them to the ground and slammed his mighty foot into their skulls. Two of the three creatures swooped down and attacked the scareman, who was hastily stripping the keys from Clot's still body. The scareman sensed the creatures behind him and rolled over, shooting the shotgun into the air. One of the creatures wiped blood from his mouth and throat and dropped like a dead bird to the stone floor. The other creature managed to knock the shotgun from the scareman's grasp. The last creature flew as fast as its wings could move for the exit, only to have Leo leap up and wrap his shackled chains around its neck.

Across the dungeon, a creature persisted in his desperate attempt to kill the scareman, who tried to use his hands to cast spells but could not, for the creature began to beat him with its rotting hands. Achilles raised his left arm, and several small arrows popped from his forearm. The creature flew up and began his final descent on the scareman, but three arrows flew true and struck the creature in the chest and neck. He fell and began to crawl. He felt a foot on his back and turned his head to spy only the barrel of the shotgun pointed at his fanged jaw. The gun blasted, spraying black blood and shards of bone across the floor. Achilles looked at the scareman in disbelief.

"I don't understand. Why the lies... Why did you do this?"

"Because, am I not a liar?" the scareman continued. "I couldn't get us into the castle without us all being immediately captured. I had to figure out a more intelligent plan. I am the smartest in the land after all..."

Achilles was filled with joy. "So, what is the other part of your plan?"

The scareman produced the keys.

"Did Leo know of your actions?" Achilles asked.

"Yes, indeed, but I was getting pretty damned nervous for a moment there." Leo smiled.

"I just cannot believe it was all a glorious act?" Achilles said.

"Yes, indeed!" the scareman said. "You see, the night we arrived in the Diamond City, and all had retreated to bed for the night, I used my magic to summon the witch. I told her of our plan. I told her of Dorothy. That's why she knew where Dorothy was and was able to send her creatures to capture her. The next night, when all had gone to sleep, I summoned the witch and told her of our plan again. This way I could ensure us at least making our way inside and winning her favor. She has gained much strength after studying my book, and I knew we could not ever make it inside the castle unless she allowed us in."

"So, she knows the dwarves are coming at dawn from the north."

"Well, not exactly... I told her they were coming from the east and planned to attack at midnight. The witch then sent a third of her troops away, thinking they could head off the dwarves."

"Brilliant... just brilliant," Achilles said in delight and great relief.

"Now we just have to find Dorothy, get your book, and get out," Leo said. "Hey, did you like the part where I spit on you? I mean, that seemed really real, huh?"

The scareman grinned. "Yes, that was a nice piece of improv on your part. Now, let's get Dorothy and try to find my book. Without it, I can't send Dorothy home or find a way to vanquish the witch." He then looked at the shotgun. "Though, I believe that this weapon would kill her. Its powder is unlike that of any element in our world." He took several shells from his pocket and reloaded. "The bad thing is the sound, like thunder! I hope this deep in the dungeon the blast was muffled."

Leo walked over to a pile of dead villains and grabbed a sword and a small shield. "Okay, let's find that trouble-making girl," he said with a devilish grin.

# CHAPTER 23

## "THE GLORY OF AN EARLY VICTORY"

The Necro Lord turned his head as if he heard something, a boom, a strange sound, but then glanced out a window as the rain was beginning to pour and loud thunder rolled across the land. He had heard several echoing booms the last few minutes, but the skies and thunder outside eased his mind of anything out of the ordinary.

The witch looked down at her sister strapped to the table. "It's finally over. I have quashed the rebellion, and by dawn, the dwarves will be gone for good and all."

The Witch of the West let out a sigh. "Yes, it's finally over. A rebellion you knew nothing of and had to think over about less than two days is finally over. You always carried such drama."

The witch laughed and pulled out Dorothy's phone. She pushed a few buttons.

"I won't kill her. She needs to teach me how to use this portable magic mirror... I think it's a machine also. Very odd. This looks like some sort of game. I thought it was her allies... but it's only something to amuse yourself. Very amusing!" she said with a longer laugh and a wide grin.

"What did we do to you?" her sister asked.

"I told you, nothing, and that is why you will be the last to die! Do you remember?" the witch said, violence and fury in her eyes. "You never included me. You neglected me, and so I had no option but to make sure you paid attention to me one way or the other. You are to blame!" she screamed. "Only the scareman valued my talents, treated me as someone special..."

"Oh, and you treated him so well. Face it, Sister, *you* are the problem, not us. You treat anyone close to you horribly!"

The witch tapped the screen. "This is actually a wonderful game... Why the woman is in white and has such large breasts is beyond me, and why is the witch the villain?" She clicked and watched the screen. "Bah! Look, I took another tower!" She screamed in delight as she showed the phone to her sister. "It says I have reached level seven, and I am getting stronger and stronger!"

The Witch of the West looked over at the Necro Lord, who turned to the window.

"Are you going to kill me now?" she asked calmly but firmly.

"I thought about it," the witch said and clicked the phone. "But I think I will let him have you... Think of the magic and power he can drain from you in the Great Mountain."

"Oh, his lair of death and horror?" the Witch of the West mumbled.

"Well, I guess... it's nothing like my castle, but it will do the job. Oh, look! I killed a wizard and reached level eight! This is wonderful! It's like conquering without all the drudgery and work." The witch shook her head and turned the phone off. "Enough for now. Take her to your lair and do as you wish. She still has much essence to draw on if she has held on to life this long. I will bring you the bodies of the dwarves from the battle soon. I have never considered her to join my army of the resurrected dead. Maybe her magic can aid you however. Though dwarves are such a moody and uncontrollable group. Enjoy the lair, Sister; it is not as nice as this castle... but it will be a suitable holding place for however long he lets you live!" She laughed and walked from the room.

The Necro Lord took his hand and placed it on the table as his dark eyes studied the Witch of the West. "We will have such fun together. I can hardly wait," he said with a wide smile.

She simply stared back with unequivocal disdain. "And to think I shared my bed with you just four hundred years ago. When did you fall from such beauty? I remember when you were so strong, tan, those piercing blue eyes, a young and very talented wizard in training. Now look at you," she said with disdain and disgust.

The Necro Lord said nothing.

The Witch of the West said nothing more.

The Necro Lord sneered as he said, "You would not stop talking when we shared so many things, and now you are silent?"

"You want to know why our love failed?" the Witch of the West asked. "You yearned for power. Your jealousy of the scareman ruined him, and in turn it ruined you, my once beautiful man." She turned her head. "I can't even look at you. Your sight now sickens my very soul."

The Necro Lord stood and let out a piercing whistle. Three creatures flew to the large window.

"Take her to my lair... Be careful with her," he bellowed.

The creatures surrounded the table as the Necro Lord stormed from the room.

# CHAPTER 24

## "A NEEDLE IN A HAYSTACK"

After several minutes of dimly lit torch-filled hallways as they dipped into the shadows to avoid randomly placed guards, the three would-be rescuers found themselves in a long, well-lit passageway.

"We cannot keep looking like this," Leo barked.

"Well, I have not been in this castle for several years. It's very difficult to remember every room and hideaway. Everything looks the same," the scareman said with a sigh.

"Maybe we should have her dog try to sniff her out?"

"Bah. If I can't smell her, no canine can," Leo remarked. "Besides, this castle is huge."

"Well, we checked the dungeon, the courtyard, and several lower floors. I would assume she would be kept higher up in a tower, or near a tower," Achilles suggested.

"True," the scareman answered. "Let's try the north wing and let her dog take a walk around. He may have some luck—besides, he can outrun the soldiers and creatures if trouble starts."

"Agreed," Achilles said.

Leo shook his head. No dog could out-track him. This quest was getting too uncertain for his liking.

They crept with a delicate grace past several guards who were gathered in a dining hall feasting on the remains of some poor animal and minutes later arrived at the top floor of the castle. The scareman placed Dorothy's backpack on the floor and called Conan over to it. The dog let out a whine and sniffed it. "Good boy. Now go find her," the scareman said with a smile.

The Rottweiler let out a small yap and blazed off down the hallway.

"There is no way he is going to find her," Leo grunted.

"He is smarter than he looks, my fanged friend," the scareman said. "Now, we must be very careful. I know within this area of the castle lies the witch's living quarters. We have to be extra cautious and hope they believe you are still imprisoned."

The wizard spoke too soon; the loud clanging of a bell began to ring out!

"Damn! She must have decided to check up on us," Leo snarled.

"Well, at least we're far from the dungeon. She and her hordes will be down there for at least a few minutes. That will buy us some time," Achilles said.

The three warriors quickened their pace, stopping at every door and peeking inside. They reached the top of a long stairwell only to find yet another hall filled with paintings and wooden doors.

"Blast, where is that dog?" Leo mumbled in despair.

They began to check each door slowly until suddenly they heard a sharp bark. The three warriors ran down the hall with great haste and turned the corner. Conan stood up, his paws scratching against a wooden door. They heard Dorothy call out to her dog, and the rescuers ran to the door.

"Dorothy!" Achilles shouted. "It's us!"

"Achilles?" Dorothy let out a sigh of relief. "Please get me out of here!"

The scareman lightly pushed Conan down and looked through a small window near the top of the door. "Any guards with you, or are you alone?"

"No, they left me. Every few minutes, two or three of those resurrected warriors look in, but they come and go."

Leo looked down at the latch on the door. A heavy lock held the door. It would take great force to be overcome.

"Achilles, I think we need your talent for picking a lock..."

Leo and the scareman stood back as the iron general smashed the menacing lock from the door. The force was so great the handle was torn off as well, and the door swung open with ease.

The first to run in was Conan, who met Dorothy still chained and began an assault with his tongue on her fair but battered face.

She laughed at first and then began to cry. "Down, boy, down!" she ordered.

Leo pulled Conan back from his master as the scareman and Achilles looked at the chains around Dorothy's hands and feet.

"Well, you could try breaking them, but you may break her as well," the scareman noted.

"I can be gentle if need be," Achilles said confidently.

One by one, the iron general very cautiously snapped the chains around the young woman's hands and feet. Dorothy hugged Achilles and the scareman.

"Thank you so much for coming back to save me. She is as evil and crazy as you said. We have to get out of here. That lady is freaking nuts!"

Leo joined in the celebration as a tear formed in his eyes. He pulled a rag from his leather belt and handed it to Dorothy. She began to wipe her tears. "How are we going to get out? Do you have a plan?"

"Well, the scareman had a plan for us to get in but…"

The scareman cleared his throat. "I am hoping we can lie low until the dwarves arrive, and amid the confusion, we will manage to sneak out. But the witch knows I have tricked her now, and we are being searched for even as I speak…"

Dorothy walked over to the table, grabbed her purse, and gathered her personal effects. "She still has my gun, but I don't think she has figured out how to reload it. She has my cell phone, too. I bet she is using the battery up playing that damn game!"

Swiftly the small group left the cursed room and began to make their way back toward the stairwell. Just as they turned the corner to the steps, they were greeted by a horde of resurrected dead. The foul warriors stood in formation—three lines of five troops. Their growls and hisses made Dorothy shudder as the two groups looked at one another.

Leo let out a fierce roar and dashed forward. Surging into the battalion, he swiftly knocked several enemies to the floor. Achilles followed and, using his great strength, tossed the remaining battling corpses to the side. The heads and arms of the defeated were scattered across the floor as the scareman and Dorothy scurried past the small skirmish. Conan made sure to do his part, leaping on a soldier and ripping its arm clear off its shoulder joint. When the dust settled, Leo and Achilles stood triumphant, shin high in bones, flesh, and armor. Even Conan looked pleased with himself as he raced over to Dorothy.

"Conan, spit that out!" she ordered.

The dog whined and just slobbered on the old bone. Leo stripped the dead for small parts of leather armor that could fit his massive frame. He then sifted through the blades and axes until he found one he could use. He was more than ready for battle.

The scareman made his way to a nearby window and looked out into the open courtyard. He slowly began to reload the shotgun and studied the moonlit landscape as his fingers placed shells in the gun until it could hold no more.

After a quick lock and load, the scareman looked at Dorothy. "We have to get my book back if you want to go home. We could try to escape and come back or attempt to get it now."

Dorothy rolled her blue eyes. "So even if we escape and live another day, I may be here for good..."

"Unfortunately, that is how it appears."

"I don't think we have much choice; we will never get another shot like this. I say we go for broke."

Leo and Achilles regrouped with their friends, Leo looking back at the carnage to which he'd contributed, smiling.

"We may have to separate and go looking for the book," the scareman said.

"Few in number is unwise if we should come across the queen," Achilles said.

"We can create more confusion if they can't find all of us, and if some of us are captured, we can at least hope the others have a shot at the book," Leo noted.

"I don't know. It's like a horror movie out there, and it seems less than wise to separate," Dorothy said and began to wrestle the bone from Conan's slobber-filled jaw.

"Give me the bone, Conan!"

The dog was not letting up without a struggle.

"Okay, listen, what if Achilles and I go look for the book?" the scareman suggested. "Leo and Dorothy lie low and wait for dawn."

"I'm not sure if sneaking around is gonna be easy. Achilles is not really built for stealth..." Leo grunted.

"I just think Dorothy needs a better bodyguard than Achilles or I. You are the greatest warrior of us three, correct?" the scareman countered.

A little fire to the ego was all Leo needed.

"Well, yes. That's a good point," he said.

Achilles rolled his eyes. "As much as I want to stay with Dorothy, the scareman is right. Leo, you must protect her. We will all meet back in the courtyard in three hours' time. Book or not, when the dwarves arrive, we flee and head for the cover of the forest."

"Agreed," Leo said.

"Good luck to you and stay well hidden," the scareman said. "Take your hand weapon and backpack as well, Dorothy. When I retrieve my book, I will need both hands for the magic I will cast."

Dorothy took the fully armed shotgun eagerly. She slid her small pocketbook into her pack and threw it over her shoulders.

"Luck has nothing to do with it," Leo boasted. "As long as she is with me, you have nothing to worry about, of that I swear."

Dorothy smiled at the courage of the lion king, held up the shotgun, and looked down the sight.

"Okay, let's move out," Leo barked.

The scareman and Achilles crept their way down the stairwell as Leo and Dorothy traveled back past the broken door. Conan watched as both couples broke away and then sat back on the floor, gnawing contentedly on the bone.

"Conan... come now!"

The slobbering dog finally gave in and slowly trotted back to his master, the bone still in between his teeth, however.

# CHAPTER 25

## "HIDE AND SEEK"

The twin moons sat at bay in the dark, cloud-coated night. Time seemed to be frozen in a vast void of horror as Dorothy and Leo waited in the shadows. Every few moments, Dorothy would gaze out a nearby window and see the beauty of the two moons. There would be a noise, and swiftly the two renegades, along with Conan, would travel on through the shadows. After several attempts to stay hidden near the top floors of the castle, they found themselves on the lower floors. They found another dimly lit corridor and began to walk quietly, listening for any noises from the enemy.

"This is getting very old very quickly," Leo growled softly.

Dorothy let out a sigh. She looked down at her watch and discovered only an hour had passed.

"The dwarves will be here in two and a half hours. I fear this castle is too huge for Achilles and the scareman to find that book."

"Well, I am going insane just hiding. What about you, kid?" Leo said with a mischievous smile.

"Well, then. Let's look for it, too," Dorothy suggested. "I mean, how many rooms and halls have we ducked in and out of in our attempt to hide?"

"You have a point," the lion king replied.

They continued walking until they arrived at yet another door.

Leo slowly opened it and quietly peered inside.

Darkness.

Leo looked down the hall.

Dorothy began to walk up the stairs as Conan dared to dash ahead. Leo trailed behind. This was getting out of control. "Damn... the scareman better find that book and kill that witch. There is no glory in dying this day. No glory at all," he mumbled.

Dorothy swallowed hard at his words. He could leave anytime. Go back to the woods. He had nothing to gain, only everything to lose. He hated the witch as much as the others, but was wise enough not to take her on. It would be only a couple more hours until the dwarves arrived to create the perfect diversion for their escape.

Why would someone like Leo risk so much for her? He didn't show much appreciation for friends and had been bitter ever since they met. Maybe he fed on hate. Either way, Dorothy's eyes began to tear up as she determined to hold on, be strong, for them all. She could feel his resentment. If they were going to die for her, she should be able to do the same. This wasn't earth or home. The rules were different here, and she had to step up and be as brave and as strong as Leo, Achilles, and the scareman.

Leo caught up to her. "Are you okay?" he asked.

"Yeah... I'll be alright. I just wanted to go home so bad, I didn't think of what it could cost you all and how selfish I was being."

"Nothing wrong with wanting to go home, Dorothy. Someday I will find a new home, a new kingdom, a new mate. Sometimes life drags you down hard, and you get angry with everyone. That's what life can seem like at times, one rough day after another…"

"I know, but why do you seem so angry, and if you hate being here with me, why help?"

The lion king stopped. "Listen, I am just not a people person… I guess I live my way, my rules. But when I saw you with Achilles and that bag of straw, I thought this girl is different. There is something that you possess, a spirit, and I was reminded of all that was good in this, or any other world. All of us want the witch dead for our own reasons, but I think we just have a different way of going about things. Don't concern yourself with my complaining. Eventually, I would have arrived here and tried to kill her and most likely failed… It's not you as much as it is me and my attitude. It's just the way I am."

"Maybe we should do the sensible thing and stay hidden as much as it bores me," said Dorothy. "Let's go find a room to wait this whole mess out until the dwarves arrive. When they get it, we will see plenty of chaos. Maybe even some rest."

Leo smiled. "We will let Iron Head and Straw-face find the book."

Leo, Dorothy, and Conan disappeared into the shadows once again.

# CHAPTER 26

## "BATTLE FOR
## THE AGES"

Alone guard stood near a hulking iron door. His eyes glazed with a dull heat. He was content just to stare at the burning torches that lit the hall. He had no knowledge of the scareman, who stood several yards around the corner.

"One guard..." the scareman whispered.

"Do you want him or should I?" Achilles asked.

The scareman grinned, a hint of evil in his eyes. He stepped into the hall and began walking with a mild strut. His arms swung lightly. The guard was slow to respond, but still he raised his bony arm, which held a small hand axe. It let out a low groveling rattle.

The scareman raised his hands and pointed his gloved hands at the creature.

"*Hetltun...*" he whispered with a smile.

The guard froze and suddenly shook. His arms tore apart like worn rope, and his bones began to crack. Throwing his head back in a deep lurch, the guard let out a small whine and fell to the floor. In seconds, a pile of bones and leather armor rested in front of the doorway as white ashlike powder floated above the remains.

Achilles took the corner quickly and caught up with the scareman. "I see you're remembering some of your more deviant spells."

"Ah yes... using what little magic I have is restoring my memory piece by piece. Reading Dorothy's schoolbooks as well."

"I hope you can retain those precious memories if we run into the witch."

The scareman placed his soft hand on Achilles's massive shoulders. "If I get my book, I will destroy her."

The scareman slowly opened the iron door, which sent a small creak into the hall. Achilles stepped in quickly with his axe held high, ready for trouble. He looked around the room quickly, but no sign of the enemy was to be seen. The room was very lavishly decorated with rugs and fine jewels strewn across the room. Pillows and velvet blankets were placed neatly in the corners. Sacks overflowing with gold were stacked against the far wall. A small wooden door to the left had several hooks that held several beautiful chains of gold and necklaces. In the center of the room was a tall thin pedestal made of wood, decorated with rubies, diamonds, and emeralds.

On the sparkling stand was a book.

The scareman ducked under Achilles's arm and walked in eagerly.

"Ah ha!" he said. "A treasure amongst the treasures."

"I don't think that is the book you seek... This is all too easy," Achilles said.

"Nonsense, I owned it, same cover and blue worn ribbon. It was a part of me, and it will be with me once more."

"Stop, Scareman!" Achilles demanded.

The scareman stopped short and angrily turned around to eye the iron giant. "What is it, you rusting behemoth?!" he asked, as his eyes burned with rage.

"Do you really think she would leave that book with only one guard and with her treasures?"

The scareman thought for a minute. "Well, since this would be the last place you would look, yes, I do. She is overconfident."

"You want it too badly. You are not thinking. That cannot be the book of magic. I sense a trap!"

The scareman threw up his arms. "Listen, we have snuck around for two hours. This is it; I'm sure of it!" He then walked over to the pedestal and stared at the heavy book.

"Ah, see? The cover reads *'Tundun shan hastooh,'* or 'Ancient Ways of Knowledge.'"

"I just think she would guard it better," Achilles added.

"See, that's the beauty of it. No one would ever go for her treasures, and if they got in, they could not read this thing and would think it was just a dusty old book. Mortals want gold and jewels, not an old worn book."

The scareman smiled as he slid his hands around the book and lifted it swiftly from the pedestal. He placed it under his arm. "See, not a problem."

Suddenly, a bell began to clang, and several nets fell from the ceiling, covering the scareman. Achilles ran to him and began to pull on the rope netting, but even he could not snap it. It looked like ordinary rope but would not break like straw.

"I cannot free you! The rope must be cursed!" he shouted.

"Then flee; get out! Find Dorothy and Leo!" the scareman said as he looked at an open window. Across the castle ramparts, he spied several of the resurrected dead running toward the treasure room.

"Get out; there is not time! Find the others and flee! I will find a spell in here and free myself! Flee now!"

Achilles hesitated. Retreat did not come naturally to him, but after hearing the commotion outside the window, he took the scareman's advice. His hulking body lumbered to the wooden door, and he squeezed his way through. He closed it swiftly behind him and found himself in a small, dark passageway. The walls were closer and the ceiling smaller. He had to get down on his hands and knees to move. He paused at first, fearing for the scareman, but then continued down the dark passageway. When he felt he was far enough from the door, he snapped his finger and thumb, and a small flame lit from his thumb like a candle. The first thing he saw was the skull of a previous thief, surrounded by several bones.

*Obviously this tunnel is not traveled often,* he thought, and under a light as small as a lit match, the iron general once again continued ever forward.

The scareman sat quietly under the nets and laughed. "As soon as they barge through that door, I am going to send them into the abyss."

He clutched the book and grinned. He watched the door swing open as two creatures and the resurrected dead poured in like water bursting from a dam. They surrounded him instantly. The scareman smiled and delicately opened the book.

The pages were blank.

He flipped them quickly, his eyes scanning the pages. Not one spell anywhere. He was tricked and trapped. In anger, he slammed the book closed. He looked at his bloodthirsty enemies and gritted his teeth.

"That whore!" he snarled.

# CHAPTER 27

## "TUNNELS OF
## TERROR"

The sound of the bell clanging would wake the dead, but not the lion king. Dorothy and Leo had found a small room deep in the south wing of the castle and hid among old pieces of armor and furniture. Dorothy shot up quickly at the sound, thinking it was an alarm clock, but Leo rolled over and let out a snore. She quickly grabbed Leo and shook him violently. He woke with a jump, and his hand swiftly shifted to his sword hilt.

"Something happened. A bell was sounded," Dorothy said.

"I bet one of our friends was captured, or the dwarves came early!" Leo said. He dashed over to a nearby window. Below he saw guards scurry to the courtyard.

"Well, it looks like something big happened, but I can't see what from here. If they've been caught, we're all in trouble, a mountain of trouble."

Dorothy walked over to the door covered and blocked by chairs and odd pieces of furniture. She began to pull a small table back.

"What are you doing?" Leo asked.

"We have to see what's going on! If they have been caught, we have to come to their rescue!"

"We are not doing anything until the dwarves arrive!" Leo shot back.

Dorothy sat the chair down and then sat on it in frustration. She looked around the room, her foot tapping as thoughts of captured friends raced through her mind.

Leo walked over to her and lifted her face with his mighty pawlike hand. "Listen, let's just sit still for a few minutes more. Maybe we can see something from the window... At least when the dwarves arrive, we can rescue our friends."

Dorothy sighed and stood up. "Yeah, I know you're right."

She made her way over to a long bookshelf and began to slide her hands past the several dust- and cob-web-coated books. Leo plopped down on the empty seat and folded his arms, letting out a small yawn.

Conan rose from his nap with a stretch.

"Your animal is ready for battle," Leo joked.

Dorothy's eyes read the different titles of the worn books. She was hoping to find the one book that could send her home. Leo became anxious and made his way over to the window once again and stared into the courtyard that seemed to overflow with excitement. Conan stood next to his master, and his ears twitched as he stared at the bookcase.

Suddenly there was a loud thump from behind the bookshelf!

Dorothy stepped back and watched as the books trembled. Conan let out a small bark.

"Leo, the bookcase!" she called out.

Leo swiftly leaped from the window and drew his blade, ready to square off with whatever confronted them. "Get behind me, Dorothy!" he ordered.

Dorothy slipped behind the lion king. The bookcase slowly began to turn and slide into the wall, and as it disappeared into the darkness, two looming eyes peered out. Leo growled and tightened his grip on his sword. There was a small snapping sound, and a light lit up the darkness.

There was Achilles on his hands and knees, his candle thumb lighting the darkness.

"Achilles!" Dorothy shouted with joy and relief.

Leo sighed and put his sword back into its sheath.

The iron general let out a small laugh and slowly crawled from behind the secret corridor. "I have crawled through this tunnel looking for a way out and luckily found a small lever on the wall." He stood up and looked at his two friends. "This is good luck indeed!" He then blew on his thumb, extinguishing the flame.

"Where is the scareman?" Leo asked.

"I bring bad news, I'm afraid. He was captured trying to get the book. I didn't want to leave him, but he insisted, and we were outnumbered. He claimed he would be able to free himself, but I fear it was all a trap. We must do all we can to find him!" Achilles said in desperation.

Leo raised his eyebrow. "Try to find and rescue him? In this castle ... with the entire witch's army alert to our presence? I don't think so."

"Well, I will not let him die," Achilles said with a stern tone to his gravelly voice. "If you want to escape when the dwarves attack the gates, you can, but I will not leave him to her Vile Bitchiness. I know what she will do to him, what she did to me for all those years... I would rather die than know I walked away from a friend and a comrade."

Leo walked over to the tunnel and looked down into the darkness. "So where does this passageway go?"

"I do not know. It may go forever through this castle for all I know," Achilles said.

"Maybe we should sneak around in it. I bet we could find the scareman, or at least hear what is going on," Dorothy suggested.

"Sneaking around would be far better than sitting here. Besides... we would have the element of surprise if he has not been able to free himself," Leo noted.

"Well, if we go, I need to be oiled... My joints ache awfully from crawling so far."

"Getting soft in your old age, eh?" Leo joked.

"Hardly, Lion King," Achilles stated. He then reached down to his massive thigh and opened a small compartment. He pulled out a small flask of odorous dark oil and began to rub it on his knees. "This should help. Now, we will need a torch. My own flame light is sadly running low of fuel."

"Dorothy, here, this is yours."

Achilles handed Dorothy the shotgun. She checked how many shells were left and slung it over her shoulder.

Her hand slid to her pocket.

No phone.

"I hate not having my phone! How much time until the dwarves get here?" Dorothy asked.

"Close to dawn, so in about an hour," Achilles said.

"Well, we better get moving," Dorothy said as she began to move the furniture from the door.

"I'll grab us some torches." Leo walked over to the window as the courtyard was now unnervingly empty.

"We better get moving. I have a feeling this castle is gonna be crawling with guards very soon."

Death surrounded the scareman. The faces of the resurrected dead and creatures grinned, evil with hunger. The guards had removed the magic nets, thrown the book to the floor with a thud, and chained the scareman's hands tightly behind his back. He held his head high, however. He was no longer afraid of the creatures or the resurrected dead, and while the witch was treacherous, the one creature he wished to not see more than anything was the Necro Lord. Anyone with that much dark magic combined with a complete lack of scruples would find it natural to torture and torture for all eternity. He was a hack. He was not as strong as the scareman, but with the darkest magic behind him, he was certainly dangerous.

*If I only could get my hands on that damn book!* the scareman thought. *I could send that hack magic user back to whatever rock he crawled out from.*

The door slammed open, breaking the scareman's thoughts as he stared down the witch as she walked in with a confident strut. The Necro Lord followed close behind, his covered head down and arms folded in his flowing black tattered robes.

The witch approached the scareman, but his eyes remained locked with hers.

She stood just inches from the scareman.

The scareman broke eye contact for a moment to glance over the witch's shoulder in a desperate attempt to see the face of the Necro Lord, but his loose robes hid his face from view.

"And so, I have ended any chances of success for you, my traitorous old friend," the witch began with a smile.

The scareman himself grinned in defiance.

"You want your book?" the witch continued. "You think you can destroy me? This was simply a feeble attempt to regain your power. Oh my." She smiled once more. "How delightfully ambitious."

The scareman said nothing.

"I will find the others... The girl is free, but it will make no difference in the end. I will have them all, just like I have you, my sweet."

"They're no longer here. They fled into the night. I alone came for my book."

The witch let out a laugh. "Oh, don't belittle me with such lies... I am better than that... and you were, once."

"The plan was to rescue the girl, and the girl was rescued. The book I sought for my own gain."

The witch turned to the Necro Lord.

"Bring him to the dungeon, and deal with him as only you can. Break him, whatever it takes. Then take him to the courtyard. I have a sweet surprise for him... if he survives the dungeon."

The Necro Lord bowed in respect, then rose, and stretched out his hand, or what was left of his hands—bony fingers with thin dark skin hanging free. Several of the resurrected dead immediately stood to attention. They grabbed the scareman and led him out of the room. The Necro Lord followed behind.

"Kill me yourself. Do not let this hack use his weak tricks and games on me! You are stronger than he is. Have the nerve to do it yourself!" the scareman shouted.

"Oh no, he can play with you first. I know how much he will enjoy it and how much I will enjoy hearing all about it," said the witch.

The Necro Lord walked past the creatures and glanced over to the scareman. The scareman still could not see his face, but he could feel the smirk from beneath his dark hood.

"A hack!" the scareman yelled. "I lost my flesh, but you lost your soul!"

The witch bent down, picked up the book of magic, and smiled. She flipped through the empty pages and laughed once more.

"Kill the witch and save the world!"

"Oh, good. I think I took another village." The witch placed the book under her arm, pulled out Dorothy's cell phone, and tapped it with her pale finger.

"Move this army here, my spies here, and my fire archers here... Excellent," she said and slid the phone away.

# CHAPTER 28

## "OUT OF THE SHADOWS"

Leo and Dorothy loomed through the stone corridors of the tunnel. Achilles, due to his massive size, crawled behind them. Every few feet, the tunnel would grow smaller and then open back to its normal size. The small torchlight cast several ominous shadows on the cobweb-coated walls. Every few minutes, the adventurers would come across a peephole or a lever to open a hidden doorway. They decided against leaving the tunnel after witnessing several guards search rooms and castle hallways. It would only be a matter of time before someone would think to search the tunnel, as well. After several minutes, they came to what looked to be the end of the passageway, at which they discovered an iron door with heavy locks.

"It looks like someone doesn't want anyone going there," Dorothy whispered.

"Or anything getting out," Leo added.

The small group stood near the door, listening for any noise.

"Do you think it holds a creature?" Dorothy asked.

"I really don't wish to find out," Leo said. He then kneeled and sniffed the air that blew through the bottom of the doorway. "But I can smell dirt and fresh air. It could be a way out, perhaps..."

"You mean a secret exit or entrance to the castle?" Achilles suggested.

"I bet this thing runs out under the mountain and into the forest," Leo said with a smile.

"Well, Achilles, you are the locksmith... Let's see if you can get this door to open," Dorothy said with a smile.

Leo and Dorothy squeezed by Achilles, and he crawled to the door. He first grabbed the iron handle and squeezed it; it broke off.

"Great," Leo growled.

Achilles looked back. "Do you wish to try?"

Leo rolled his eyes and looked away.

"I didn't think so," Achilles said. He then leaned his massive weight against the door, which began to groan and bend. It slowly began to crack; Achilles slowly raised to one knee and then pushed again. There were sounds of metal snapping and the creaking of iron, and suddenly Achilles fell through as the door flew open. Achilles looked up to see walls of dirt and stone. The tunnel was much larger now, and he was able to stand tall. Leo and Dorothy joined him in what appeared to be a cave. Conan ran ahead but stopped short with the light of the torch. The ground below them was now cobblestone.

"Well, now what?" Leo grumbled.

"We push on," Achilles said.

The dark cave was filled with stalactites that jutted from the ceiling. They walked on farther, watching the shadows dance as they came upon a set of stairs of slate and clay.

"After you," Dorothy said, smiling at Leo.

"Not a problem." He pulled his sword from its sheath and led the group down the stairway. Achilles continually watched his footing on the small steps.

"I would assume this was once a cavern for mining gold. I wonder if this is the work of dwarves?" he asked.

"I wouldn't doubt it. They dug into every mountain they could find," Leo said. "I had to throw them off my land twice, and that was with a treaty!"

They arrived at the bottom of the stairs.

Achilles's hunch was correct.

Before them were several wooden wheelbarrows, broken and covered in cobwebs. Some old iron tracks lay buried in rubble, and tools coated in dirt and clay were scattered everywhere.

"She probably took this cavern right before the battle in the Forest of the Damned," Achilles noted.

"Well, then, there must be a way out!" Dorothy said with a smile.

Leo and Dorothy walked in different directions and looked for another tunnel. Leo found the remains of a few tunnels, but unfortunately, they had been blasted shut. Rocks of all sizes covered their way out. "Well, we could try digging our way out," he suggested, "but it may just lead us deeper into the mountain."

Achilles walked over to the lion king and eyed the size of the rocks. "The dwarves would have arrived by the time we made any progress."

"True. We should head back through the corridors and try to find the scareman. When the dwarves arrive, we can make our escape."

Dorothy came running from the shadows excitedly with her torch in one hand and shotgun in the other. "Guys, come see what I discovered!"

They followed Dorothy around a pile of rocks and found themselves in a large room with rock walls and lit candles all around. They stood at the entranceway, looking through the room. Dimly lit as it was, they could make out a large thronelike chair and a small desk.

On the desk sat a book.

"I bet that's the book!" Dorothy said in delight. She swiftly ran into the shadow-coated room.

"Dorothy, wait!" Leo shouted.

Dorothy arrived at the desk and looked around, suddenly realizing how foolish it was to rush in.

Leo gritted his teeth. "Don't touch the book! It could be cursed!"

Dorothy peered into the darkness and then used the torch to see the book.

"I can't read it... It looks like Latin or French!" Dorothy said.

Leo slowly crept into the room, looking to his left and right with each step.

"Okay, listen... if we must, then we must grab the book and run for the stairs. All we need is for a wall to come down or some horrible beast to be let loose..."

Achilles stood guard at the entrance. "Do it with great speed!"

Leo arrived at the desk and looked around into the shadows. "Okay, Dorothy. Place the torch on the ground... when I count to three, grab the book and run like mad to Achilles. I'll cover you."

"Are you sure?" Dorothy asked.

"I am not sure of anything anymore, but we must take the chance that this is the book! If so, we may be able to kill the witch, use it to get Scareman back, and send you home."

Dorothy nodded. She placed the torch on the ground.

"Okay then... one... two... three!"

Dorothy's right hand trembled as it hovered above the book. At three, she swiped it off the desk and ran as if the devil were chasing her. Achilles and Leo ran also, not looking back.

The only sound as they ran, however, was that of their beating hearts. After several minutes, the adventurers had made their way quickly up the stairs, past the destroyed iron door, and back into the tunnels of the witch's castle. Leo and Dorothy collapsed to get their breath as the iron general turned and peered back at the tunnel.

"Okay, no traps?" Dorothy said, gasping for air.

She looked at the book.

"I hope this is it..."

"Does it contain a blue ribbon?" Achilles asked.

"What?"

"The scareman mentioned it held a blue ribbon," Achilles said.

Dorothy turned the book and prayed for a blue ribbon. "Yes, blue ribbon, weird lettering. Let us all hope this is the book for the lives of us all. Should I open it?"

"No!" Achilles and Leo shouted in unison.

"Okay... it shall remain closed," she said as she staggered to her feet and placed the book in her backpack.

# CHAPTER 29

## "I MUST BREAK YOU"

The scareman lay on a wooden table, his hands and feet bound in heavy gold chains. He looked to the ceiling, wondering what the Necro Lord had in store for him.

Suddenly, the dark hood of the Necro Lord appeared over the scareman. He then pulled back the hood, revealing what lay beneath. The scareman cringed. The skull-like face of the Necro Lord was badly scarred as thinning white hair attempted to somehow form a beard and mustache. His black eyes glared at the scareman.

"I gave my flesh, too, you arrogant self-loathing coward! The darkness eats what remains of my flesh every day. But it also heals me. You claim to be so righteous, your cause, your magic, that damn book... I do not deserve the book, but you do? Your skills are pitiful compared to mine!"

The scareman turned his face away. "Well, you do have the breath of a rotting corpse, of that I am certain."

"The witch is strong, but I am stronger. The dark arts have revealed to me the steps toward eternal life... and power you can only dream of."

"I did not want to live forever. I did not want to rule over others. I simply wanted to save magic and not let machines take away its awesome beauty. Speaking of beauty... could you replace your hood? Your face disturbs me."

The Necro Lord spat in the scareman's face and stood. He adjusted his robe and slid his hood back, covering his face once more. "The magic of the Black Mountain has delivered more power than you, even with your damned book. I will never play second string to anyone ever again!"

The scareman looked around at the several guards. With his hands bound, he was powerless, but if he could free his hands, then perhaps... Suddenly, he saw the Necro Lord slide his hand over his straw face, and the burning began. The scareman screamed in horror as the intense heat began to burn his clothed head. He thrashed and wailed, and the Necro Lord stopped abruptly.

The dark creature then spoke. "Nothing clever to say now? Funny how flesh burns... but straw burns so much easier."

The scareman gasped for breath and looked around. "Okay, I admit that was pretty painful. I would prefer you to refrain from doing that again, if possible."

"Tell me where the others are, wretch. Tell me your plan."

"I told you the truth. I don't know where they are! They left! That was the plan."

The Necro Lord slid his hand over the scareman's leg, and it glowed red with heat, and the burning began once more. Screams the scareman could not contain bounced off the walls.

"I cannot fully burn you, as I have to bring something of you back to the witch. She wishes to destroy you herself."

"Just bring her my heart because she destroyed that years ago!"

The Necro Lord chuckled. "Ah yes... true love, one of life's greatest weaknesses." He slid his bony hand to the scareman's neck; smoke began to rise from the scareman's cloth mask. He screamed and screamed as his neck and head began to scorch.

"This is rather fun," the Necro Lord said. "Oh, how I wish I could take you back to my lair for more..."

"I wouldn't be so sure of that. I think killing children is all you can manage. A grown wizard like myself may present more of a challenge. Why not unchain me and fight me, or are you a coward as well as a psychopath?"

"You would like that, but I have my orders... so talk!" The Necro Lord grabbed the scareman's shoulder, and fires began to burn his arm.

"I swear I do not know where they are!" the scareman screamed in agony. Exhausted, the scareman could only move when the pain struck at his very soul. After several more attempts, the Necro Lord pointed at the chains that held the scareman, and the guards released the scareman. His body was limp as they held him and kept him from dropping to the floor below. The Necro Lord looked into the scareman's eyes.

"Your mind is strong. I can feel your magic protecting you, but nothing can protect you from the witch's scheme." He pointed to the door. "Take him to the courtyard!" the Necro Lord ordered.

The guards obeyed, and the scareman was dragged from the dungeon.

After hiding amongst the shadows once again, the small band of adventurers found themselves high on the walls of the castle.

"We have to get closer to the ground. Even if the dwarves arrive, we must make it to the gate."

"I know. I am working on a plan," Achilles answered. His eyes scanned the castle walls and then out into the woods that rested quietly several hundreds of yards away. "For now, we must wait here for the dwarves' arrival."

"We still haven't rescued the scareman!" Dorothy said with concern. "We can't just leave him!"

Leo stood and walked over to Achilles. "If you want, I can try to find him alone. You must remain to protect Dorothy."

"You would risk your life for him?" the iron general asked. He then thought for a moment and glanced at Dorothy, who slid the shotgun from her shoulder to her hands.

"Even if we do escape, none of us could send Dorothy home," he remarked. "Without the scareman's magic, she will be stuck here forever."

Suddenly, there was movement in the court-yard below.

"Look!" Dorothy said.

Leo and Achilles glanced over the wall as several of the resurrected dead began to arrive in the courtyard. A dozen creatures flew from several windows of the castle and joined the resurrected dead. Their screeches and howls sent a chill down Dorothy's spine.

"Something is up..." Leo snarled.

Trees emerged from the castle next, their dying limbs reaching out, thrashing, and clearing a path.

A figure stumbled from the castle, chained to a wooden cross. His head hung low, and he struggled as he dragged the end of the cross.

"Scareman!" Dorothy whispered with great sadness.

The scareman continued to stagger as several of the resurrected dead taunted and hissed behind him. Some carried torches while others cracked whips over the scareman's back.

The witch now emerged with the Necro Lord behind her. The rows of her minions parted as she strode ever forward, but the heckling of the scareman did not let up for a moment.

"Holy shit!" Dorothy muttered.

"This is very bad," Achilles said. "The dwarves will not be here for several more minutes."

The adventurers continued to watch as the scareman made his way slowly to the center of the courtyard.

The creatures began chanting, and the scareman slowly turned around to face the witch. He made eye contact with her and then stared with fury at the Necro Lord. The witch simply smiled widely.

"Put him up!" she ordered. Two tall, thick trees scurried forward, wrapped their limbs around the scareman, and lifted him into the air. Several more ran to the spot underneath the scareman and began digging like dogs. After the hole was deep enough, they scampered away, and the hulking trees slammed the end of the cross into the hole.

The scareman was hanging by his arms as the cross leaned a couple of inches to the left. Several of the resurrected dead then approached and grabbed his legs, wrapping them in chains. Once he was secured, the witch and Necro Lord walked to the cross to give their last respects.

"You could have had it all: glory, power, my body each evening, and I would have turned you back into a man. But you chose to make me a fool. Now you will see what I do to traitors." She spat at the ground and turned away.

"You are nothing but a whore of lies!" the scareman shouted. "You caused the rain, you bitch! You used my book. You threw the world of magic into the darkness and damned the world of machines. You have destroyed our once beautiful world, damning us all!"

"What difference at this point does it make? You were the one person in our land I feared, and after you are gone, I will rather enjoy crushing all, butchering their children, and then setting my sights on lands beyond my own."

The scareman didn't move. At this time of great trial and suffering, the scareman remained stoic and defiant.

"I don't like the look of this," Dorothy said in alarm.

"Where are those damn dwarves?" Leo barked. "They must be very close by now!"

The witch looked at her small army and smiled. "Enough fun... Archers!"

A dozen resurrected dead archers lined up yards from the hanging scareman. They pulled bows from behind their shoulders and armed them with arrows. Another lit a small torch and slowly walked down the line, setting the arrows alight. The scareman did not flinch, however, but stared with disdain at the witch.

"Oh my God!" Dorothy said. "We can't let this happen!"

Leo looked down at the courtyard thirty feet below. Dorothy grabbed Leo by the shoulder. "We have to do something!"

"Like what? How are we going to save him? There is a veritable army down there, and we're up here!" Leo grit his teeth, deep in thought for a moment as he slid his paw over his sword sheath. "What can I do?" he whispered, his mind racing.

The witch began her count. "Ready... aim..."

The archers focused on their victim. His dark eyes watered but were fueled with rage, not pity.

"Fire!" cried the witch. The scareman stared at the witch. He would not give her the pleasure of witnessing any cowardice on his part, of that he was certain.

Suddenly, there was a thunderous crash!

The ground shook!

The archers fell, collapsing into one another. The wooden cross tilted. Two arrows sailed through the air...

Achilles, however, stood square in front of the scareman. He turned his back as the arrows struck his iron body. They bounced off and fell harmlessly to the ground. Leo and Dorothy looked at one another and then at the great leap Achilles had made. Achilles wasted no time and lifted Sun Seeker.

"Die, Witch!" he cried as he hurled Sun Seeker like a lightning bolt. The massive weapon sailed across the rows of resurrected dead, decapitating several of them in the process. The axe sliced through everything in its path.

The witch was stunned and had just enough time to fall to her left. As she did, she grabbed in desperation at the cloak of the Necro Lord, who stumbled and fell to her side.

The axe missed the witch but found a new target and lifted the Necro Lord by the shoulders and chest, pinning him to the stone wall. His body shook, and he cried out in anger and despair as black and purple ooze sprayed like a fountain across his upper body and neck.

He shook with a tremor and then hung still.

Achilles looked over at the scareman. "We lived as enemies, but today if we die, we die as allies and comrades for all time!"

The witch scrambled to her feet. She looked back to the Necro Lord, his robes coated in the glossy ooze.

"Kill them!" she ordered with a shriek.

The resurrected dead began their assault, flying into the iron general, who batted them away one after the other.

Dorothy pulled the shotgun and aimed down into the masses. "Damn it!" she cried and began trying her best to get a shot at anything.

Leo ran down the ramparts and found a set of stairs. He flew down them, sword in hand, and charged into the courtyard.

"Looks like this gladiator has one more show to put on!" he shouted and ripped into the courtyard, swinging at anything that moved.

Dorothy fired several shots down into the courtyard, which confused many of the resurrected dead as they were struck and thrown to the ground. The witch watched in horror as the resurrected dead began to scatter. With the Necro Lord dead, they had no control and began to stumble this way and that. Leo began crushing the walking corpses with fury as Achilles ripped down demons from the sky. Dorothy, seeing her chance, quickly scurried down the stairs and ran straight to the scareman.

She looked up at him. "How's it hanging?" she joked.

"Get me down from here!" he shouted. "No time for your world's horrible humor."

Dorothy leaned on the cross with all her might, but it refused to budge. "Achilles!" she yelled.

The iron general tore his massive axe from the stone wall as the Necro Lord's corpse collapsed in a puddle to the ground. Achilles looked over at Dorothy. He thundered across the courtyard, knocking creatures and resurrected dead to the ground. He arrived at his hanging companion and wasted no time, dropping his axe and using his massive hands to slowly yank the cross from its earthy grasp.

Dorothy suddenly ducked as a creature flew overhead. Achilles set the scareman softly to the ground. He then began working the chains and ropes that bound the brave warrior. The scareman let out a sigh as freedom was unleashed. Leo continued his wild attacks, dodging tree branches and leaping at the resurrected dead.

Conan added to the excitement, running aimlessly and barking wildly.

The scareman stood and looked at the mighty Achilles.

"Thank you, my friend," he said.

The iron general let out a grunt. "You said I plan too much? So... this is how it feels to improvise? I must say I rather enjoy it! What a rush!"

He ripped Sun Seeker from the ground and raised it high into the air. "Come at me, you sons of sapless whores!"

Dorothy looked over at the scareman, who shrugged his shoulders.

"Not my first choice of battle cries..." Dorothy commented. "He is trying."

Dorothy began reloading her shotgun and then pulled out the worn book from her backpack.

She handed it to the scareman. "Is this what you were looking for?"

The scareman's eyes lit up as his shaking hands reached for the book.

"Yes... yes, indeed!" His voice trembled.

"Hope you are a fast reader 'cause we got company, and they seem uneasy to say the least..." she added.

Achilles charged and slammed his axe into the nearest tree. It spit chips of wood, and sap sprayed into the air as the tree cried in agony.

The witch ran swiftly to a small landing and watched in horror as the last of the resurrected dead collapsed under the sword of the lion king as he swung and swung in fury.

"Crush them! Burn them! Stop them! Kill them!" she cried.

Several more creatures and human guards poured from the castle with axes, whips, and swords. Dorothy took aim and fired. This sent them scattering.

In all the noise and chaos, the scareman flipped through the pages of the ancient book, his eyes scanning the pages. A flaming arrow flew over his head, but he did not flinch. His mind raced as the spells he once knew began to come back to him. Achilles stayed busy in a wild furor as more trees emerged with a hunger for destruction in their eyes.

Leo was filled with alarm as several guards took aim with crossbows and then fired. The arrows pierced the air with startling speed and yet suddenly stopped just inches from the lion king! They hung in the air and suddenly turned the way they had come and found new targets. The guards moved too slowly as the arrows hit their marks. Leo looked across the courtyard as the scareman walked confidently across the battlefield. He raised his left hand and snapped his fingers. A tree that stood in his way shrieked as it ripped in half. Leo grinned and ran to meet the scareman. Every beast then ran to attack the scareman, but found itself crippled and withering on the ground in seconds.

Suddenly there was a massive thumping sound on the drawbridge!

Dorothy ran to the scareman and Leo.

"The dwarves are here!" she yelled.

Outside the gate of the castle, a small army of dwarves and humans sent a battering ram of logs into the door.

"Onward ya lousy dwarves... Put your backs into it," Brawner ordered.

The battle outside the walls of the castle had begun. Several of the creatures and evil trees ran to the door to await the enemy. Dorothy watched as the witch retreated up the stairs and back into the castle. "She is making a break for it!"

Leo growled. "Let's finish this!"

The band of warriors made its way past the oncoming hordes, the scareman using his magic to protect them from arrows and blades and Achilles's axe sending the closest attackers to the ground in agony. They arrived at the stairs, and with Leo leading the charge, the group pursued the witch with great haste, vengeance in their hearts.

Outside the castle walls, the screams of evil creatures and the howls of angry dwarves rumbled. The humans lit up the sky with flaming arrows, causing the trees to scamper in chaos. Several of the witch's army soldiers were fleeing in terror as more and more it seemed certain that they were facing defeat, which gave heart to the warriors. Brawner instructed several squads to throw ropes over the castle walls and tie them to nearby dead trees. They had to get the drawbridge open if they were to take the castle. They did not have the time or power for a long siege.

The battles continued on the ground and in the air as creatures swooped down and ripped dwarves from the ground and flung them into the foul, water-filled pit. The dwarves met a gruesome death as the bloodworms ripped them apart. The dwarves fought on, however, sending many of the remaining resurrected dead into the pit with them.

Inside the castle, the band of Dorothy, Leo, Achilles, and the scareman charged on, full of hope and adrenaline through the dimly lit corridors of the witch's stronghold.

"When we find her," Achilles boasted, "I will have her head!"

The scareman did his best to read and stay up with his comrades at the same time. He shook his head angrily. "You cannot kill her. She is magical, and nothing in our world can harm her."

Dorothy tightened her grip on the shotgun. "I bet this would put a hole in her," she said with confidence.

"That may be true, but we won't know until we find her..." the scareman shot back.

They followed the hall to a winding set of stairs and slowed their furious pace. After they reached the top of the stairs, they found a large archway that entered into the roof of the castle. They then saw the witch; her back was turned. Suddenly the doorframe was blocked by a massive trunk of a tree.

Black Root shoved his body through the doorframe, knocking bricks from the archway.

He stepped slowly toward the group. "I will rip you apart with my powerful branches!" he bellowed.

Achilles pushed the others back as a massive armlike branch raked across the air, striking a nearby wall. He lined up Sun Seeker, but several roots suddenly wrapped around his legs and tossed him to the cold stone floor. A branch then ripped Sun Seeker from his grip. Black Root pulled Achilles close and began to crush him with his branchlike arms.

"I wonder what this weapon would do to you, almighty Achilles?" the demon tree teased. He tossed him to the floor, and the castle shook once more. The tree then came forward and began to swing Sun Seeker.

Achilles rolled out of the way of the weapon's blows and pulled the chainsaw from his leg compartment. Black Root lifted Sun Seeker high and swung down, eager to split Achilles's iron skull, but the hulking machine sidestepped and pulled the cord on the chainsaw.

Black Root was still wondering how he had missed as he looked down.

Achilles sank the chainsaw into the mighty tree's side as the blades cut deeper and splinters of wood and black sap sprayed from Black Root.

Black Root fell backward, and as he did so, Achilles swung the chainsaw once more, pushing it deeper and deeper as Black Root cried out in agony.

Dorothy put up her hands as black sap sprayed everywhere. "Gross," she mumbled.

Achilles stepped toward the fallen tree and looked deep into its black dying eyes, the chainsaw still sputtering and sending smoke into the air. He dropped the chainsaw, picked up Sun Seeker from the ground, and lifted it high above his head.

"Say something cool before you kill him!" Dorothy shouted.

Achilles's helm was coated in black sap. He looked down at Black Root's face, writhing in agony.

He then leaned in and shouted, "Something cool!"

He slammed Sun Seeker into Black Root's face, splitting him in two. He took a moment for himself before he stood up, yanked the giant sap-coated axe from the dead tree, and walked back to the others.

"Okay, that was pretty cool, a bit meta but still cool," Dorothy said. "Kinda funny, too."

"I cannot believe you made the machine worse than he already was. Now he speaks like you! And what the hell is 'meta'? Your world is very strange," the scareman said as he shook his head.

"Oh relax, Scareman. It was 'pretty cool' if I should say so myself!" Leo barked.

They headed toward the ripped-out doorframe to the tower. They could see the witch near the edge of the castle with only a few guards near her.

"This ends now!" Achilles growled and tightened his grip on Sun Seeker.

Leo, being the swiftest, wasted no time and charged in and howled. The witch turned, but her face revealed no fear as a host of nets sprayed into the air, and the lion king ended up on the floor, tangled like a fly in a web.

"Damn his lack of patience!" the scareman cursed. Achilles and the scareman ran to help their friend when suddenly three massive trees stepped from behind a hidden entrance and charged the two warriors. The scareman was knocked to the floor, and Achilles struck one tree, but the others soon used their mighty limbs to wrap around him.

Conan ran around barking and causing some disturbance, but a creature swooped down and sent the dog into the near wall. Dorothy took aim with the shotgun. As the tables began to turn, the witch cried out, "Enough!"

Dorothy began to sweat as she took aim.

The witch just smiled and slowly walked toward her. She eyed the barrel of the gun. "You realize, girl, that if you shoot me, your friends will all die."

Dorothy thought for a second, a second too long, as a creature swooped from behind and knocked her to the floor. The shotgun slid toward the witch, coming to a halt just a yard from her feet.

The scareman let out a cry as several of the resurrected dead picked him up and began to beat his straw body. Achilles stood helplessly with his iron body wrapped tight in limbs and roots. Several creatures now untangled Leo from his nets and pinned him against the ground. One held a dagger across his furry throat.

Dorothy scrambled to her feet and quickly found several spears and swords surrounding her.

The witch picked the shotgun up. "So, I see you liked my little trap?"

Dorothy looked at the blades and her friends helplessly.

"You didn't think it would be that easy, did you?" the witch began. "Oh, and for your little friends outside... my army to the west will be arriving back any moment. The minute you escaped, I sent for them. It was a valiant effort, but that is all it will be remembered as."

The witch grabbed Dorothy by the throat and smiled.

Outside, the melee continued. Brawner ripped his axe from the chest of one of the resurrected dead when he saw the forest move. "What in the blazes?" he whispered.

Kilian looked toward the double moons, and several dots appeared. Brawner squinted his battle-worn eyes. "Reinforcements for the witch!" he cried.

The witch's forces had returned. The valiant fighters were now greatly outnumbered. The dwarves huddled together with the humans and formed a defensive circle. Gloom filled their hearts. Everything they had fought for would be in vain.

The first wave of trees surged from the woods as the human archers' fiery arrows found their mark, sending the demon trees retreating. The first wave of creatures, however, thundered down with screeches and began ripping the humans and dwarves apart.

Brawner looked as two dwarves climbing the castle walls were attacked and dropped into the pit. He looked to the castle wall and prayed to Harnan, the dwarven god of war, for one last fight before he joined his brothers in arms.

The witch let out a small laugh and walked over to the castle wall as creatures filled the night air.

"Fools... all for nothing. They will all die. But not you, girl. I have special plans for you." She handed the shotgun to a nearby creature and walked over to Dorothy. "You will live for a long, long time as a reminder of what happens to those who dare attempt rebellion."

The scareman lay exhausted on his stomach and watched as the witch began her verbal assault on Dorothy.

"They will all die," the witch continued, "and I will make you the greatest example of my power."

All eyes were on the witch as the scareman began to quietly chant. The witch's boastings were loud like that of a horn, and so her guards did not hear as the scareman continued his spell. He took his one free hand and pointed toward the trees holding Achilles.

"My dear, we have a saying..." the witch said with a grin. "Never anger the witch. Besides, you're just a girl..."

Suddenly, the scareman shouted the last word of his spell, and a fireball exploded from his arm. He screamed in pain. The ball of flame slammed into the trees, and Achilles was free. He looked around as the demons began to step toward him. He pointed his darts and fired, not at the oncoming enemy but toward Leo's captors.

The creatures pierced by the darts fell from Leo as he locked eyes with the creature holding the shotgun. He lunged with all his strength as the witch watched on. The creature let out a war cry, but Leo slammed his paw across its jaw, knocking the beast to the floor. The shotgun fell, and Leo rolled to it. He leaped up, holding the weapon, and hurled the gun across the floor until it lay at Dorothy's feet. The world stood still. Dorothy smiled.

"We got a saying back home, too..." she said as she picked up the shotgun and aimed the barrel at the witch. "Life's a bitch, and then you die!"

She pulled the trigger, and a thunderous boom echoed across the rooftop. The witch shook for a moment and looked down at her chest. Her royal clothes were in tatters, and blood and smoke seeped from her body. She started to open her mouth as Dorothy took aim again.

A second burst of thunder filled the air. The witch stumbled back and leaned against the small wall of her castle, blood pouring from her lips. With one last effort, the witch lunged at Dorothy as a third blast sent her back once more. This time she stumbled and fell, watching in despair as her hands began to turn to dust. The witch staggered to her feet and tried to launch one last attack. She collapsed to one knee and then the other, however, as her body continued to crumble.

"I curse you, false prophet. You are not a savior or hero to anyone. You're nothing!" the witch screamed, her words slurred and broken. The witch fell back into the wall and sat gasping.

Dorothy walked over, kneeled, and lifted the witch's head as her chin began to break off into dust in Dorothy's hand.

"I want my phone, bitch..." Dorothy whispered.

The witch's head collapsed into ashes in Dorothy's hand.

The witch was dead.

Dorothy stood and looked around. The remaining resurrected dead began to collapse. She reached into the witch's black dress, covered in ashes, and found her cell phone. She smiled. It still had 20% left in the battery. She slid it into her pocket.

Dorothy ran to the scareman, kneeled, and began to help him up, but his right arm was gone from the elbow down. The smell of burned straw hung in the air.

"I thought you could not use fire magic?" Dorothy whispered.

"I could, but I always feared it would destroy me."

"But you said you couldn't use it... all this time?"

The scareman let out a laugh. "I guess I lied. I am a liar, after all."

Leo joined Dorothy. There came a large rumble from the skies as the clouds began to break apart, and the twin suns shone through the early morning sky. The trees began to scream as the sunlight pierced their dark eyes. They cried out as they turned to stone. Achilles, using a short burst of power, broke free from the grip of the tree as it transformed.

He joined the others. "The witch is no more!" he screamed as he raised his massive metal arms to the air in victory.

Light pierced the dawn's sky. It was something neither dwarf, nor man, nor any other living creature had seen for nearly a decade.

The small twin suns shone brightly.

The creatures were horrified, and one by one they screeched as they began to burn. Some fell from the sky; others just thrashed on in agony. The humans and dwarves on the field of battle covered their eyes as the light blinded them. The remaining demon trees fled into the forest, hoping to hide from the suns' light, but to no avail as they slowly began to turn to stone. On the rooftops, human guards dropped their weapons and kneeled, bowing their heads to Dorothy and her fellow warriors.

The curse of the witch was broken. The four heroes walked to the wall and looked at the ragtag army, who thrust their weapons into the air and shouted, "Victory!" over and over.

Dorothy blushed, Achilles stood proud, Leo blew kisses, and the scareman smiled.

"I never thought victory would be so sweet," Achilles said.

"That's 'cause you're not used to it," boasted Leo. "Hang around with a champion like me, and you will see it gets better every time."

Dorothy rolled her eyes and laughed.

"Well, now, all we have to do is get you back home," the scareman said over the chants from below.

Dorothy looked down at the trees, and slowly green life began to bud. The mud-caked ground and yellow blades of grass began to change as well, and the air became fresh and sweet.

"Let's go down and greet our admirers," Leo growled with a smile.

Dorothy just laughed. "Leo, they are not admirers. They're part of our team... There is no 'I' in team, you big jerk."

Leo snorted and grinned. "But there is an 'I' in win!" His ego would not fail him in his finest hour.

The rest laughed and began to drag Leo down from the wall.

"Let's go," Dorothy said, and they made their way from the rooftop back into the castle.

Brawner greeted Achilles and the scareman.

"We sent word the witch is dead. All the gem cities will hear of this battle and that her reign is truly over. A celebration greater than any in our history will begin, and we will feast!"

"How long will it take you to find a spell to send me home, Stitch-face?" Dorothy asked.

"As long as it takes to celebrate and look upon the world that you saved," the scareman said softly as he watched the people celebrate.

"Fine, I'll stay a couple days. But I need to get back. I have family that needs me, and I need them."

"Fair enough. I will find the spell and send you home after a few parties."

Dorothy smiled and hugged the scareman. "Thank you for sending that tornado to bring me here."

"Well, I really didn't do that either," the scareman said. "I was trying to save myself; those dwarves almost had me."

Dorothy shook her head. "You are such a liar!"

"Yes, indeed, but no longer... I think these humans and the dwarves could use my help. We can make our world better than it was before the witch came to power. I can see now that magic and machines can benefit our world."

"Wait, follow me. Achilles and Leo, you too. This is what we do to celebrate back home."

They followed Dorothy to the remains of the witch and stood over them.

"Now we urinate on her remains, right? Mark our victory!" Leo said with a wide smile.

"No!" Dorothy took out her cell phone. "We take selfies."

"What?" the scareman asked.

"We take pictures, like we did before. Okay, get close. Achilles, you will have to get down in the back."

The group huddled together as Dorothy took several selfies. She looked at her battery. It was down to 10%. She showed them the pictures.

"That mini magic mirror is amazing," the scareman said.

"Some technology is very helpful. Now, let's go celebrate," Dorothy said as the heroic warriors walked toward the brave humans and dwarves.

The Necro Lord stumbled to the cave entrance of his lair. He crawled in and collapsed. He rolled and lay still on the cold floor. There was no one to aid him now. His breath was short and labored.

"Oh honey, you're home!" came a sweet voice.

He looked over to see the Witch of the West standing tall in a flowing white gown. A large hawk rested on her forearm. "I do not know what happened, but suddenly the guards fled, and I was freed. Anyway, I just thought

I would make myself at home, and the children cannot wait to play with you…"

"The children?" the Necro Lord asked.

He was fading fast; the magic of the Black Mountain could only give so much.

"Yes, silly, the children. Now that you are going to be dead, you can all play together for eternity."

From behind the Witch of the West, several small shadows of white appeared.

"No wait! Please help me. I promise I have learned my lesson!" the Necro Lord begged.

One of the children stepped up and hugged the Witch of the West. "He can play with us now?"

"Yes, little one, he can play with you forever and ever in the Magic Mountain."

The little girl stepped up and looked at the Necro Lord. He could hear his heart slowing, his body fading.

He looked at the girl. She was so innocent…

"Rip and tear…" she said sweetly.

From behind the Witch of the West, three dozen more children appeared. "Rip and tear!" they shouted.

"Kill that poopy head!" shouted a little blond boy.

"Put him on the table of woe!" shouted a young girl.

"He has stinky breath and a booger face!" screamed another.

Their hands began to rake against the Necro Lord as his ghostly form was taken from his dying body. The children grabbed his ghostly figure as he kicked and fought in panic. His shrill screams echoed in the caves.

"Rip and tear!" they shouted again.

The Witch of the West walked to the cave entrance.

"It's my lair now, you poopy face!" She laughed and looked out over the land as the suns shone and grass began to grow.

# CHAPTER 30

## "UNTIL WE MEET AGAIN"

The land, once overpowered by death and darkness, was born anew. A new land full of color and light and fresh air celebrated the witch's death and the return of the suns. Trees filled the rolling hills with several shades of green, and flowers clustered in the seas of rolling green grass. There were birds once more, chirping and singing in celebration.

The Diamond City, once clouded in darkness and stone buildings, was slowly returning to its previous glory; the Ruby and Emerald Cities also began to return to their former glory. The humans worked alongside the dwarves, cutting lumber, stone, and precious gems to rebuild the great capital. Word was sent to the Land of the Lions, and ships with supplies and workers to aid them were on their way.

There was a renewed sense of hope in this once-dead land.

As for Dorothy, as much as she had come to love her new friends and comrades, it was time for her to return home. A great banquet was planned for the afternoon amid a celebration of dwarves, humans, and lions.

Dorothy was torn. She longed to remain, but was very worried about her aunt.

She took one last look at the sparkling buildings and, with Conan at her side, made her way out of her room down into the busy streets below.

The streets flew banners and advertised the afternoon events. Dorothy walked past several onlookers who cheered. She arrived at the tavern and found the scareman looking through his book. Brawner and Killian were with him.

"Well, I hope you found that spell," Dorothy said hopefully.

The scareman looked up. "Yes, indeed. You will have to use the machine you arrived here in, though."

"I don't think it's in working order," Dorothy said.

"Oh no, girl. We repaired it, so it is as good as new... Well, maybe not that good, but good enough to get you back," Brawner said with a wink.

From the street, several dwarves pushed Dorothy's truck. They had fixed the dents and scratches, even the glass. It was not perfect, but it did not look as bad as it had when overturned in the Forest of the Damned.

"Not bad," Dorothy said.

"It's the least we could do," Brawner said.

"And what of you, Scareman?" Dorothy asked.

"Me? Well, I cannot find the spell to return me to my human form, and being a one-armed wizard, I may not be as powerful as I desired, but I think in tandem with the dwarves and Achilles our talents can make our world much better for all."

"Very true. Find common ground and work up from there."

Just then Leo, along with Achilles, arrived with the sound of cheering echoing in the streets.

"Well, it's about time you rolled out of bed, Dorothy," Leo teased.

"I have been up for a few hours, actually," Dorothy said with a smile. "I can't express my love for you all... but I'm needed back home."

"Well, while you slept, Achilles was voted commander of the new Gem Cities, and I must return to the Isle of the Lions. A new treaty has been drawn up, and we will be rebuilding my kingdom with the aid of the humans and dwarves."

The streets were filled with humans and dwarves, all in bright colors, as the suns sat still in the blue sky. Dancing, laughter, and sweet relief filled the air.

"Dorothy, we should go. It's time to send you home, dear friend," the scareman said.

They climbed into the truck, and Dorothy turned the ignition. It started the first time. The scareman sat in the passenger side. "Those dwarves can fix anything!" he said. "Let's get you home, child."

Dorothy began to drive with Achilles and Leo in the back, as the truck was covered with flowers and confetti. They arrived at the gates of the Diamond City, and Dorothy parked the truck several yards away.

After instructions from the scareman, she climbed out of the truck to say her goodbyes.

"This part sucks, but I have to return," she said.

She then hugged Achilles, then Leo, and finally arrived at the scareman. "You know, you were a real jerk when we met."

"I do not know what a jerk is, but I agree. I think I had a lot to learn about how to treat others," the scareman said.

"I have learned how much I need good people around me," Dorothy replied. "I thought I could do everything on my own, but life is not meant to be spent alone. Life should be a journey with friends... With friends, you can overcome any obstacle."

"I think we all learned such a lesson," the scareman said. He pulled a small blue vial of liquid out of his pocket and handed it to Dorothy. "This will help you sleep and rest, so the journey will not be so hard. It is a tornado, after all."

"Good. I do so hate heights." Dorothy pulled the cork and drank the potion. The taste was like a blue popsicle. She handed the vial back to the scareman. He then set his hand on Conan and whispered, *"Kreachundan."* Conan whined and fell asleep.

"We can't have him feeling the ride either," said the Scareman. "Now put those straps on yourselves and close your eyes."

Dorothy buckled herself and Conan into their seat belts and looked once more at her friends. "I will never forget you," she said with tears in her eyes.

"We will always be in your heart," Achilles answered. The scareman then turned and walked back to the others. Dorothy closed her eyes, and the scareman began his spell. He raised his one arm in the air, moving it in a large circle. Dorothy opened one eye and saw her friends waving as the wind began to blow around her. Suddenly, she could no longer see, and as hard as she tried, she could not hold her eyes open, and she slowly fell asleep.

Achilles looked at Leo. "Did you remember what to put in her backpack?"

"Come on, I am not that forgetful..." said Leo. "Not like the scareman."

The scareman let out a chuckle, and his spell worked its magic as the truck rose high into the air.

# CHAPTER 31

## "WHERE AM I?"

Dorothy's body tingled, and her eyes opened as she heard the whine of Conan and slowly sat up. She was dazed but found enough strength to place her hands on the steering wheel. Conan lay on the floor of the cab. Dorothy looked out the windshield, now cracked, looking like a giant spider's web. There were shouts, and suddenly the door was ripped open.

Dorothy turned to see Officer Rollins.

"Are you okay, Dorothy?" he asked.

Dorothy didn't respond right away; it was all too much to take in. Finally, she replied, "My dog, where is Conan?"

"He's safe in the cab," Officer Rollins said as he carried Dorothy from the wrecked truck to the road a few yards away.

"A ferocious storm hit, and we received a report saying there was a twister spinning a truck high in the air."

Dorothy tried to stand up, but just fell over.

Just then, Adam pulled up in his truck and ran out to help. "Everything okay?" he asked.

"Yeah," Henry replied. "Dorothy got railed by that twister."

"Conan?" Dorothy asked again.

Still wondering what had happened, Adam ran to the truck and lifted the beefy dog out. He whined and whimpered.

"Jeez, Dorothy. You got lucky," Henry began. "That tornado must have hit you and then headed right for the town. People are in shelters; the power's out almost everywhere."

Dorothy stood up and saw an ambulance approaching. "I didn't leave? I thought I went to another place..."

"Well, I am sure you did. In that damn twister, it's lucky you came back safe and sound," Henry said.

"No, I was in another land. There was a witch and dwarves and..."

"And monsters and magic spells," Henry joked. "You took quite a ride in that truck. You must have one hell of a concussion."

Dorothy looked at the truck, yards away in the dying cornfield. Its front end was crushed, and broken glass and twisted metal covered the body.

Adam put down Conan. "I think he is okay, just shaken up a bit."

Dorothy looked around, confused. "It was all a dream?"

She squinted, and the sun took her by surprise as Officer Rollins continued, "Dorothy, I want you to relax. Take deep breaths. Does anything hurt?"

"Yes... no... Listen, I am fine. I just need a minute. I had this dream and I..." She looked at the truck and at Henry, Adam, and then the one-armed farmer who was walking over with a first aid kit.

Her mind was still trying to put things back together as a black convertible screeched to a halt. It was Miss

Harris. She glared at Dorothy and pulled down her sun-glasses. "Poor girl. You should know better than to drink and drive."

Henry stepped up angrily. "Madam, this is a police and medical situation, and that twister is what threw her off the road."

Miss Harris smiled. "If you insist, officer," she replied as she returned to her car.

The convertible sped off as Dorothy stared at it all in disbelief and much confusion.

"She's a witch!" Adam said.

Dorothy's head sank slightly.

"Dorothy, we're going to take you to the hospital in the next town over," the one-armed farmer said.

Officer Rollins helped Dorothy to her feet and took her to his squad car. He helped her slide in as she sat.

"It was all a dream. Just a damn dream…" she mumbled.

She felt around. "I need my phone; I need to call my aunt…"

"I'll get your phone," Officer Rollins said. "I bet it's in your truck."

Officer Rollins walked to the remains of the truck, opened the door, and looked inside. He found Dorothy's phone on the floor and grabbed it. He returned it to Dorothy as the police radio chattered with updates about the giant twister. "Just sit tight okay; we'll figure this out. We had a little warning, but I do not know how bad the town was hit. I think your aunt's place will be fine, however, being outside of town and all."

Dorothy sat back and closed her eyes.

"Kill the witch and save the world!" her phone chirped. Dorothy laughed and then began to cry.

She looked at her phone and tapped the screen. The screen opened and the photo of her with the scareman,

Achilles, and Leo standing over the remains of the witch shone back.

"What?"

She clicked the screen again. She went to her photos and found a dozen pictures of her and her friends from another world. She pushed the screen and saw a picture of the witch making faces at the camera with the Necro Lord behind her.

Dorothy began to laugh. "At least I'm not crazy."

Adam walked over and popped his big blond head in. "Are you going to be okay?"

Dorothy quickly hid the phone by her side. "Yeah, I'm good, a bit shaken up, but I'm good," she said and smiled.

Conan sat down by the door, still too weak to jump up on Dorothy. His small nub tail wagged joyfully, however. Adam walked away.

"We went there, aye boy!" she said.

Just then, the one-armed farmer walked over, struggling with Dorothy's backpack. "Here you go, kid. I didn't know schoolbooks were so heavy. Then again, I was never much into books," he said and set the backpack down in the seat. "You rest up. I'll go check on your aunt and your family's place in case your phone ain't working. Signals aren't that good right now."

"Thank you," Dorothy said. She pulled the backpack closer as the one-armed farmer walked away. She unzipped the top, found a letter on script paper, and began to read.

*Dear Dorothy,*

*Thank you for saving our world. Thank you for killing the witch. We will always remember you and your bravery in our land. As a small token, we hope these gems are worth something in your world and can help you in some way.*

*I hope the journey home was not too hard. Controlling a wind so powerful with only one hand won't be easy, but I will do my best.*

*You will always have a home and friends here. Take care of yourself, child.*

*Love,*
*The Scareman, Leo, and Achilles.*

Dorothy opened her backpack, and hundreds of diamonds, rubies, and emeralds shone from the inside of the backpack. Some were small, others the size of stones.

Dorothy sat back and quickly zipped her backpack up.

Officer Rollins returned. Dorothy stayed quiet and looked at the backpack and her phone. Officer Rollins walked around to the front seat and crawled in. The police radio buzzed.

"Hey Rollins, you best better get back into town."

"What's the situation?" he asked.

"Well, it's the damnedest thing… Everyone is fine. The only building hit was the bank! It's in ruins, nothing left, and money is flying all over the streets."

"What?"

"Yeah, it's like the damn twister came into town and just squatted on the bank! Miss Harris just drove up in her convertible. She's going crazy! Absolutely hysterical… We may have to get a straitjacket on this woman. She's a mess!" the voice on the radio replied.

"I'm on my way," said Officer Rollins.

The truck pulled back onto the small state road, and Dorothy rubbed Conan's thick head.

Small drops of rain began to hit the windshield.

"Rain? That wasn't in the forecast?" Officer Rollins mumbled. The drops hit harder, and he turned on the truck's wipers.

He glanced up in the rearview mirror and looked at Dorothy. "You're sure you're okay? If so, I just need to get to town to check on the damage, and then I swear we'll head straight to the hospital."

"No rush. I think everything is going to turn out well. Very well indeed," Dorothy said as she pulled her backpack closer. She glanced at the phone and watched as the battery fell to 1%.

She looked at the picture on her screen and smiled and then looked out the window as the blazing blue sky turned gray and the rain fell. She was so happy to welcome the rain.

Dorothy thought of her new friends, looked down at the backpack full of jewels, and picked up Conan extra tightly; she then sat back in the seat watching the rain fall with a smirk on her lips. "I killed the witch. I killed the damn witch..." she whispered with a smile.

The rain continued.

# MEET THE AUTHOR

**M**ark Tarrant was a creative powerhouse who knew he wanted to write and create from his first encounter with *Star Wars*.

Born in Lansing, Michigan and growing up in Massachusetts, Tarrant grew up loving books about monsters and the unknown.

A big fan of comics—especially those of Robert E. Howard's Conan character—his reading eventually included the master of horror, Stephen King. His storytelling was also influenced by his passion for Western movies, particularly *The Good, The Bad & The Ugly*.

His artistic talents have received recognition in *The Boston Globe*, *USA Today*, *The Valley Advocate*, *The Republican*, *The Herald*, and *The Buzz*.

Mark strove to continue to create unique characters and situations for entertainment, whether it be in film, comics, books, or short stories. His favorite two words were, "What if..." or for those who knew him, "Cigar time..."

Tarrant's personal life was a sharp contrast to the fantasy world that captivates his readers. He lived in New Mexico, loved history, especially the Wild West, and got especially excited during the NFL season.

Learn more about Mark at www.MarkTarrant.com

## Discover more at
## 4HorsemenPublications.com

**10% off using HORSEMEN10**